KEEP DANCING, LIZZIE CHU

by

Maisie Chan

AMULET BOOKS · NEW YORK

Cataloging-in-Publication Data has been applied for and may be obtained from the Library of Congress.

ISBN 978-1-4197-5992-5

Text © 2023 Maisie Chan
Illustrations © 2023 Natelle Quek
Book design by Chelsea Hunter and Becky James

Printed and bound in U.S.A.
10 9 8 7 6 5 4 3 2 1

Amulet Books are available at special discounts when purchased in quantity for premiums and promotions as well as fundraising or educational use. Special editions can also be created to specification. For details, contact specialsales@abramsbooks.com or the address below.

Amulet Books® is a registered trademark of Harry N. Abrams, Inc.

ABRAMS The Art of Books
195 Broadway, New York, NY 10007
abramsbooks.com

To all the young carers in the world

PART ONE

CHAPTER ONE

Silent Yet Deadly Buses

Saturdays were generally uneventful. A chore, even (apart from watching *Strictly Come Dancing*). But not this Saturday. No, this Saturday, Wai Gong nearly got his head knocked off by a single-decker bus—the number four, to be precise. It was one of those eco-buses that you can't hear coming. The headline would have been **DEATH BY SILENT YET DEADLY BUS**. Luckily for both of us, I saved his life, because that's the kind of granddaughter I am. It's been just Wai Gong and me since last year, when my grandma passed away, and I wasn't about to lose him too.

I was making my way home from the market; my arms were tired from carrying the shopping bags. Red lines streaked my palms where the straps dug in—I blamed the two kilos of red potatoes and the bag of jasmine rice. I was walking as fast as I could because the quicker I got home, the sooner I could sit down. My flat feet were aching badly.

As I turned into Woodlands Road, I heard the familiar sound of the Mr. Whippy ice cream truck on the opposite side of the road, waiting for kids to appear. The battery must have been dying, as "If You're Happy and You Know It" was horribly out of tune. The autumnal sun was shining brightly, which meant I had to squint to see the lump hunched over at the edge of the pavement. As I got closer, the clouds moved over the sun. Then I recognized a familiar figure.

Wai Gong was on his knees, jabbing a piece of wire through the cracks in the roadside drain like he was trying to catch a fish with a makeshift rod. His uncombed black hair hung over his face like frayed curtains; he was wearing the red scarf I had knitted him. He'd worn it even in summer, and now that the cooler weather had arrived, he was rarely without it. Grandma Kam had started it off a couple of years ago, and I'd finished it a few months ago. It was just one of the things I had taken upon myself to sort out. I liked to keep busy—it stopped me from getting too down in the dumps. I really missed my gran; she had been a mother, a good friend, and a grandma rolled into one. Now it was just my wai gong and me trying to take it one day at a time.

It had become a habit, doing the things she used to do, such as the food shopping, the cooking, and even paying the household bills. Wai Gong was so sad after she died. He refused to get out of bed, and some days he wouldn't eat at all. There were days I wanted to hide under my duvet too, but I couldn't just let him get thinner and thinner. So I made him some chicken and sweet corn soup, just like Grandma Kam used to do. I told him to get dressed in my teacher voice and took him for walks around Kelvingrove Park. It worked. He was still occasionally out of sorts, but he was closer to his old self again. Lots of people offered us help, but Wai Gong said we didn't need it, that we had each other.

The eco-bus passed me in stealth mode, silently edging toward the human shape that was my grandad.

"Get up, Wai Gong! The bus!" I shouted. But the ice cream truck's loud jingle drowned me out. "Wai Gong! It's gonna hit you!"

My heart was thumping. I rushed toward him as fast as I could, but the bags were so heavy, they slowed me down. The bus was getting closer and closer.

I yelled, "Wai Gong! MOVE OUT OF THE WAY!" He looked up and waved at me. I sped up, but it felt like my feet were sloshing through mud. The bus was just a few meters away from him. He smiled at me and yelled, "Hello, Lizzie!"

The bus was about to give his head the biggest metal kiss. That's when my body pumped into action. I dropped the shopping bags. I ran as fast as my legs would go. I grabbed the end of his red scarf and pulled it with all my might. He fell back onto the pavement, his eyes bulging as he clasped his hands around his neck. The bus sped past, BEEEPing loudly. The driver held up her fist and shouted something rude. I knew this because a mother at the front of the bus covered her child's ears.

As the bus sped off into the distance, I sighed and squatted down next to Wai Gong, both of us in shock. He was trying to catch his breath. I loosened the scarf around his neck.

"You . . . you . . . strangled me!" He rolled over onto his hands and knees, panting. "Why did you do that?" He moved the hair out of his eyes.

My heart was beating so hard I thought it was going to explode. All I could hear was the ice cream truck's happy drunken song fading as it drove away.

"That bus almost killed you!" I said, wondering if this was what superheroes felt like after they saved someone's life. Probably not. "I was trying to save . . . you . . ." I panted.

"A quick death by bus is preferable to a slow death by strangulation. What in the name of Guan Yin were you doing?" Wai Gong said, taking off the scarf and rubbing his neck.

I sat on the pavement and watched as two large potatoes were battered by a Toyota hybrid and a cyclist swerved into a lamppost to avoid riding over a very large marrow squash (which only cost me a pound) that I was going to make soup with.

Wai Gong rose to his feet. He brushed down his black joggers and peered at his scuffed brown shoes. I walked over to where I'd dropped the bags. The egg box had flipped open. Half a dozen yolks were shimmering through cracked beige shells.

"Not the eggs," I lamented. I'd hoped to bake cupcakes tomorrow for my birthday.

"Come on, it'll be all right. I'll help you get all the food out of the road," said Wai Gong. I was too tired to argue. The road was clear of traffic. We gathered most of it up and repacked it into the bags. Wai Gong walked into the road and picked up something flat as a pancake.

"This chicken is dead," he said, surprised. He held up the sad, squashed, pale poultry, then smiled. "Twice-dead chicken, a rare delicacy!" He laughed. "Do you think we can eat it?"

I couldn't help it—I began to chuckle too at the thought of run-over chicken with smashed potatoes on the side. Although the tire marks didn't look that appetizing.

"If it wasn't dead before, it certainly is now," I said. "And no, we can't eat it—it's basically packaged roadkill." I never could stay angry at Wai Gong for long. He put the chicken into the nearby litter bin. I felt bad that I'd wasted money buying a chicken only to have it pulverized by a car. I hated wasting money, full stop, and I hated wasting food even more. We had to be careful. If we spent too much, it might mean sitting in a cold house for a few days.

"Wai Gong, why were you even in the road, anyway?" I asked.

"I think I dropped my house keys down there," he said. He nodded in the direction of the grate at the edge of the road. The silver wire he'd been using stood upright like a skinny finger pointing to the grey sky.

"Oh," I said. I hoped he'd just misplaced them at home, because getting a new set of keys would eat into our weekly budget. After the rent came out, there wasn't much left. "Okay. Come on, let's go home and I'll make us a nice hot drink."

Wai Gong smiled. I noticed he had dark circles under his eyes. I didn't think he was sleeping as much as he used to.

Wai Gong took one of the shopping bags, which was now half the weight after our little incident. We walked to our tenement's front door. There were some large weeds growing next to the step that I hadn't had time to pull out. Neither had Mrs. McGuigan, who lived on the ground floor. The window boxes were full of soil with no plants growing in them, only brown leaves starting to curl at the edges that had been blown in by the wind.

I took my house keys out of my coat pocket and opened the communal door. Then we went up the stairs to our flat. Once inside, we put on our rubber slippers and hung up our coats on the wooden pegs Grandma Kam had nailed to the wall. They were slightly wonky, but I liked them that way. She'd put two coat pegs high up for her and Wai Gong, and there was a third one near my waist that she'd put up when I was about six so I could hang up my own coat. Now I used her peg.

More bills had been delivered by the mail carrier. Bills always seemed to come in beige envelopes. I shoved them into the pile of pizza flyers and other unopened mail that had gathered beside the front door. I hated opening them, often choosing to avoid them until we got the ones with angry red writing on the outside: FINAL DEMAND.

Wai Gong carried the bags into the kitchen and put on his music. This week it was "My Heart Will Go On" from that *Titanic* film Tyler's dads loved to watch. Tyler was one of my best pals, and his dads were called Antoine and George. Antoine was from Chicago, which I thought was cool, and he worked at Glasgow University. His field was meteorites. Tyler was proud that his dad was one of the few Black scholars who studied space rocks. That was probably why he loved *Star Trek* so much.

I was glad to be home despite the warbling coming from the kitchen. I put my keys back in my coat pocket and accidentally knocked Wai Gong's coat onto the floor. When I picked it up, I heard a familiar jangle. I reached inside the pocket, and there were his keys. I grinned. He'd almost gotten his head knocked off for nothing; his keys were there all along.

CHAPTER TWO

Someone to Watch Over Me

I poured the boiling water into the rainbow teapot that had a small chip on the spout. There were three random mugs in our house that also had chips. Chi, my other bestie, always said I should throw them away and get new ones. But I just couldn't. They might not have been perfect, but each one held a special memory for me. The mug with the cats on it was my favorite. Grandma Kam had bought it because she loved the dancing tabby cat in the middle. The other cats were doing catlike things, such as playing with a ball of wool or licking their fur, but the dancing tabby stood out. Grandma Kam said that cat was just like her, different from the rest. She said it was okay to be different and not follow the "other cats," even though that's what some people thought you should do. Even though it had a teeny-weeny chip, I couldn't throw it away.

Wai Gong was unpacking the shopping bags. He held up the bruised marrow squash.

"What is this? Wah, is this a giant zucchini?" he said. He held it like a green baby Hulk in his arms and started rocking it from side to side.

I nodded. "Yep."

"It's about as heavy as you when you came to us, and much cuter!" He began cooing at the marrow. "Ha! I'm kidding! You were such a quiet baby. Never cried. Kam was worried that you didn't make any noise. But I knew you were strong. Being noisy isn't always good."

"But at least I wasn't green and bruised. Don't drop the baby!" I laughed nervously. It always made me feel strange when Wai Gong talked about me as a baby; I'd come to live with them when I was just twelve days old. Grandma Kam had said, "Sometimes life is hard, but we've got to carry on." My mother had died giving birth to me. My nameless father was never found; my grandparents had no idea where to look. But I couldn't complain. I'd had a lot of love. If you had a family that loved you, that was all that counted. It didn't matter if your grandparents raised you or if you were adopted, like Tyler was. What mattered was having people who loved you.

"Kam wanted to teach you some of our favorite dances, didn't she? Before she . . ." Wai Gong held the marrow close to his chest.

I nodded. Wai Gong had a melancholy look in his eyes. He started waltzing the marrow around our small kitchen. I watched in silence; I didn't want to interrupt his moment. I could tell he was thinking about her; he had that faraway look that he'd had during her funeral. When he stopped, he gently placed the marrow on the chopping board. His hands were shaking, and he sat down at the half-folded wooden table.

I poured some jasmine green tea into the dancing cat mug and passed it to him. I wondered if he was feeling chilly and that was why he was shivering.

"Shall I put the heat on now?" I asked.

"No, no. I'm not cold. We can put it on later when we need it."

"Are you all right, Wai Gong?" I asked.

"Of course. I am always all right. Strong as an ox, I am!"

"Stubborn as a mule!" I added. That's what Grandma Kam had always added when he said he was strong as an ox. I often found myself saying things she used to say. It was my own way of remembering her.

"That I am, that I am." He sipped his tea, and his hands eventually stopped shaking.

I wondered if I should bring up the subject of his keys. Wai Gong didn't like being told he was wrong.

"Wai Gong . . . bending over the curb onto a busy road was dangerous, you know. That bus . . . it could have . . ."

12

Even thinking about it made me feel sick. My belly flopped with anxiety.

"But I had to find my keys. I'm sure the bus driver would have seen me. I'm not a little guy, you know. People think because I'm Chinese that I am weak, that I can't take care of myself. But I can. They underestimate me. Look at this muscle!" He flexed one of his arms like a body builder. I laughed, as he wasn't skinny, but he wasn't exactly the Hulk.

"No, it's not that. But you could have been hurt. You're not invincible."

"Actually, I need to look for the keys some more." He put his mug on the table and got up.

"No, wait a minute!" I said, holding my hands out to stop him. "I found them here in the flat." I ran to the hallway, grabbed his keys, and jogged back to the kitchen.

"You've got them! I knew you would find them," he said, holding his palm up for a high five. He seemed so happy that I didn't want to tell him they were in his pocket this whole time. I gave him a little pat.

"There must be a way for you not to misplace them again. I know, I can put them on this Baby Yoda key ring. Chi gave it to me, and it lights up in the dark so you will be able to see them better." I took the key ring off my house key and added it to his.

"She won't mind?" he asked.

Well, she probably would mind, because she was always trying to get me to be as fanatical about *Star Wars* as she

13

was. But I wasn't fussed about it either way, unlike Chi, who wanted to live in the outer reaches and had watched *The Mandalorian* about a gazillion times.

"How is Chi?" Wai Gong asked. "I've not seen her for ages." Chi came over a lot, but he was always out. He said he was trying to find a new job, but I knew he was mostly browsing through the CD racks in charity shops or walking around the local parks.

"She's fine, and she won't mind." My stomach made a gurgling sound. "I'll get dinner going. Then we've got *Strictly Come Dancing* to look forward to later; it's musicals week!"

"I can't wait to watch it. But first I'm going to my room," he said, changing the subject. "I need to talk to the gods and goddesses." He walked out of the kitchen.

His abrupt departure made me frown. I followed him to his room and peeked around his bedroom door. He was kneeling in front of his altar; it used to be in the living room, but he'd moved it to his bedroom a few months ago. The shiny white porcelain gods and goddesses looked down on him with glazed eyes. In the middle, Guan Yin was serene and beautiful. Her long black hair hung straight down with the front pulled up in a golden flower, flowing white material cascading over her head like a waterfall.

"I know I always ask for your help, dear beloved Goddess. But please, can you give me better luck? I promise I will bring you fresh juicy oranges next time," said Wai Gong. He held two lit joss sticks. The smoke wafted around like ghost snakes in the air.

"Please watch over Lizzie. She's such a good girl. And if you can hear me, Kam, I miss you, and I wish I could dance with you again in Blackpool, like in the old days. We had such a good time, didn't we? Tomorrow is a new day, yes. I can do better tomorrow. It will be special."

I accidentally stumbled forward and moved his bedroom door a little.

"Come in, Lizzie. I know you are out there, I can hear the floorboards creak!"

I gingerly entered his room. I saw his trio of Chinese deities. Ji Long was a god who looked after the poor. He carried a gourd and was probably tipsy because he was always shown smiling wildly. The fat buddha, Budai, was for wealth and happiness, and Guan Yin was the goddess of compassion and mercy. Wai Gong liked her the best.

"I am praying to the goddess because my fortune is very bad lately, Lizzie. I didn't get that job stocking shelves in the oriental supermarket. I have another job interview lined up though. I hope I can get that one."

I sat on his bed.

"Wai Gong, we don't use the word *oriental* anymore. It's outdated. It makes people like us sound like exotic objects.

Rugs are oriental, not people. I already told you." I was constantly telling him not to use that word, but it was hard for him to remember when other adults used it too.

"But that is what the shop is called. What else should they call it?" he asked.

"East Asian supermarket is better. Or Chinese supermarket." Mrs. Begum had told us, "Words matter." I wasn't exotic or from some fictional place called the Orient. I was just like everyone else. Chi and I were always being mistaken for one another at school even though she had long black hair and I had shorter wavy black hair. I'm Scottish Chinese, and Chi is Welsh and Vietnamese.

"Okay, I will try my best, Lizzie. You're such a clever girl for knowing these things. No more oriental from now on."

I didn't tell him that Chi and I had been called names in the street last year by some older boys dressed in black hoodies and tracksuit bottoms. They'd called us much worse things than oriental. I hadn't wanted to worry him back then, as he'd been spending a lot of time visiting Grandma Kam in the hospital. Chi had shouted back, and the leader had become sheepish, appearing foolish in front of his pals.

"Anyway, Guan Yin was looking out for me today. She made sure you saved my life and found my keys," he said, distracted. He was talking about his favorite deity like she was real. Sure, it was lucky that I had been in the right place at the right time, but she was just a figure in the stories he told me.

"I don't know why the goddess is not helping me find a job. My luck is still bad. Fifty percent bad luck. I need to pray harder to be one hundred percent lucky."

I rolled my eyes. Not again with this silly goddess stuff. Whenever something negative happened to Wai Gong, he thought it was because he hadn't given good enough offerings to his gods. He even blamed the torrential rain on bad luck; he should have known by now that this was Glasgow. It was famous for its horizontal rain that soaked your trouser legs in less than a minute. It wasn't bad luck—it was just normal weather!

"Wai Gong, wait. Before we have dinner and watch *Strictly*, will you tell me a wee story first? The one about the peacock?" It was one of my favorite tales about the goddess. Getting him to tell me his Guan Yin stories was one way to make him spend time with me.

He smiled and sat on his bed. He closed his eyes, took a breath, and then opened them wide.

"Let's begin," he said.

Guan Yin and the Brown Bird

Before humans populated the world, ten thousand different kinds of animals roamed free. They were happy and watched over by the goddess Guan Yin. She cared for them and told them how unique each of them was. They loved her deeply. One day, Guan Yin knew it was time to leave her earthly duties and return to heaven. She bid the animals farewell and ascended into the sky. The creatures lamented, "Who will look after us now?" Chaos ensued. The animals began to fight; they were confused and felt abandoned. They called out for Guan Yin to come and help them. She floated back to Earth after hearing their cries. Her compassion and mercy spread to the animals, and soon they were back to their loving and cooperative ways.

Guan Yin returned to the heavenly realm. But the same thing happened again. The animals fought, hated, misunderstood, and forgot all about compassion. Guan Yin knew she had to do something more. She gathered the animals together. Before her feet, a dull brown bird sat and watched the upset animals who were already wondering what they would do without their beloved Guan Yin. The goddess gently placed her hand on the brown bird and in an instant transformed it into a beautiful peacock. It opened its feathers wide and proud, on the end of each one an eye.

"I shall always be watching over you through this bird. Be kind, be loving, and be compassionate to each other," she said. The ten thousand animals felt relieved that Guan Yin would always be watching over them.

When Wai Gong finished, he squeezed my shoulders.

"She's watching over us, Lizzie," he said. He lay down on his bed and stared at the ceiling, then closed his eyes. I wondered if Grandma Kam was like the peacock, watching over us.

I loved listening to his Guan Yin stories. They made me feel special somehow. His parents had told him the same stories; they made me feel like I was connected to my ancestors.

Thinking about family and Grandma Kam suddenly made me sad. I went back to the kitchen and saw the empty chairs. I felt cold and alone. My eyes became wet, but I blinked back the tears. Then I looked at that marrow. There was no time for crying. Dinner needed cooking.

CHAPTER THREE

Strictly Saturday Night

"Wai Gong, are you finished with this?" I asked, picking up the tray I had used to bring him his food. He'd taken to having his dinner in his room, which made me feel a bit shut out. I didn't like eating by myself. It had been very different from when Grandma Kam was alive and we'd sit at the table in the kitchen and talk about things. Nothing very special, just regular things like how school was or if Grandma Kam had a funny customer in the bakery where she worked.

"Sure, I'll bring the tray myself. Is it time?" he asked, standing.

"It is! It's *Strictly Come Dancing* time!"

He held out his hand so I could pull him up. "What are we waiting for?" he grinned and sang, "Da da da da da da da da da da da da!"

Our Saturday nights in front of the TV were deemed

"family time" in our flat. Grandma Kam had started the weekly ritual a few years back. She'd bring back sweet treats from the bakery, and we'd eat them while watching celebrities waltz around the dance floor. I especially missed the coconut tarts with the glazed cherries on the top. Wai Gong used to work in a warehouse, but the night shift was hard, and he hated not being with us on Saturday evenings. He quit that job and got a position in a factory instead because the hours were better. But when Grandma Kam became ill, he wanted to spend as much time with her as possible and quit that job too.

We carried on having Saturday-night family time after she was gone. When we were watching *Strictly*, somehow it felt like Grandma Kam was still around.

Wai Gong sat down in the living room with a mug of hot water with a slice of ginger in it and a tartan blanket over his legs. "Come on, Lizzie, it's about to start!" he shouted. My favorite part was when the hosts said, "KEEP DANCING!" The three of us used to say it too and do jazz hands. But now Wai Gong and I didn't do that anymore.

"I hope to see a rumba! I prefer it to the salsa . . . but they're right, it's a hard dance to do," Wai Gong said.

"I'd love to see a hip-hop mash-up with a cha-cha," I said.

"Nooooo! That would be terrible, Lizzie. I hate when they ruin a perfectly good cha-cha with all that other nonsense," Wai Gong said.

I didn't realize he was a cha-cha purist, though I knew that Grandma Kam's favorite dance was the cha-cha. "Kam and I had a little in-joke back in the day that we could meet for afternoon cha! You know, because chá means tea in Chinese. We used to laugh so much because when we said the name of the dance, we were actually saying 'tea-tea'! The other dancers didn't get our humor. When I called her to meet me, I would say, 'Kam, how about we meet for afternoon cha tomorrow at the Blackpool Tower Ballroom.' We couldn't afford to have the actual afternoon tea with the sandwiches and the scones, but we would go dancing."

Dancing was how my grandparents had met thirty-eight years ago. Two Chinese people on the dance floor at the Blackpool Tower Ballroom in England back in the eighties must have been a sight to see.

"I wanted to take Kam for afternoon tea there before she . . . went. But I didn't get the chance. It's my only regret." Wai Gong turned back to the TV. I felt something harden in my chest as I imagined them waltzing around the dance floor, him holding her tight, her laughing.

The familiar theme song began playing as the disco ball sparkled in the center of the screen. Wai Gong's foot tapped as he sang, "Da da da da da da da, da da da da, hey!" I smiled. It was the one time he was truly happy. Wai Gong's eyes lit up as the hosts trotted down the curved staircase. He clapped in delight. Then all the dancers appeared like magic from the sidelines.

"Look at his hips! Oh, when I was younger, I was just like that!" he said. I laughed—I couldn't imagine my doddering grandpa being like that very cool and hip dancer. He put his bowl of popcorn on the table next to him, got up, and started to dance. I giggled; he looked like he was in a trance. He grabbed the photo of Grandma Kam and started waltzing the frame around the room, singing.

"Da da da da da da da da!"

Then he plonked himself down in his chair, ready for the group number, and stuffed some popcorn into his mouth.

The female dancers started off in feathered and sequined dresses, and then the male dancers joined in, wearing top hats and tails. They were all smiles. I noticed how their sparkly outfits caught the light. Grandma Kam had said she missed dressing up in fancy outfits. Her one wish was to go on holiday to the Blackpool Tower Ballroom and dance again. But we hadn't managed to get her there in time.

Wai Gong and I watched with glee as the celebrities and professional dancers did their thing. The one we were the least impressed by was an "influencer" called Jam4DX who had seventy million followers on YouTube. Loads of kids at school loved him and bought all his merch with their pocket money. He didn't look much older than me but was nearly in his thirties, and like me, he had two left feet.

The older politician I didn't recognize was funny and danced to a Korean pop song that had dominated the charts last year.

I didn't like that song because kids started doing the moves and singing it every time I walked past. And I'm not even Korean!

We stayed up for an extra hour to see the votes. And as I'd predicted, the influencer was out. His professional dance partner, Carmen Piernas, was one of Wai Gong's favorites. A million views on YouTube didn't always translate into votes on *Strictly*. Not only did you have to dance well, you had to have the extra "it" factor. Grandma Kam's favorite dancer, Milo du Peck, had never made it to the final round. She was always annoyed that he got put with the worst celebrity dancers for laughs. She had hoped he would win one year.

"Tonight's show was so good," I said, switching off the TV.

"It was brilliant! Those two men dancing the tango were fantastic—you never saw that in my day. They were powerful and totally in sync. I hope they stay in." Wai Gong usually had a good eye for who would make it to the final.

"Me too, they were awesome. And Milo du Peck looked very dapper in that tuxedo for the opening group number. It's a shame he was out in the early weeks of the competition, but it's great we still get to see him in the group numbers!"

"He did. I haven't worn my dancing suit for years—I don't know if it would still fit me." He patted his stomach. "You feed me well, Lizzie."

I smiled. I tried my best, but I wasn't a good cook like Grandma Kam. I missed her cooking. I tried to think of a way to return the compliment.

24

"And you . . . tell the best stories!" I said.

"I'm glad we've kept up this Saturday-night tradition. And tomorrow is going to be a fantastic day! I can feel it in my bones!" he said. He squeezed my shoulder. "I'm getting old. I'm off to bed." It was only eight P.M. He was in his sixties, which was oldish but not *ancient*. I knew what he meant though. I felt the same sometimes—old beyond my years.

"I'm sure you'll be okay," I said reassuringly. This must've been what missing someone so much did to you. "You've been through a lot. We'll work everything out, Wai Gong. You don't need to worry." He'd mentioned tomorrow being a fantastic day—it was my birthday tomorrow. A lot had changed since my last birthday, that was for sure.

I picked up the TV remote and pressed the red button. The flat fell silent. I looked around at our little home. We were doing all right. Wai Gong seemed like his normal self again. I was looking forward to whatever he had planned for tomorrow!

CHAPTER FOUR

Happy Birthday to Me

The sunlight pierced through a crack in the curtains and hit my eyes, waking me up. It took me a moment to realize that it was Sunday, and it was also my birthday. The only thing I had really wanted to do for my birthday was to make some cupcakes with cream cheese icing, but since all the eggs had broken, that wasn't going to happen. Still, I had a warm feeling in my belly.

I was now twelve and no longer the baby of my friend circle. One step closer to being a teenager! I sprang out of bed and ran down the hallway. It was eerily quiet. I tiptoed across the threadbare carpet and put my ear to the living room door, wondering if Wai Gong was waiting for me on the other side. I held my breath and slowly opened the door, eyes wide with expectation.

As I walked in, I exhaled, my shoulders literally dropping.

Nothing was different. There were no balloons. There was no Wai Gong. There was no note saying presents were hidden around the house, which was what Grandma Kam used to do. There was nothing that suggested Wai Gong even knew it was my birthday. My eyes began to sting. A concrete boulder formed in my chest.

He'd really forgotten. There were no cards or presents.

I gulped down my disappointment and walked over to the window. No, it was fine. Birthdays were overrated, right?

Raindrops were chasing each other down the dirty windowpane, and my own waterworks began, tears falling down my cheeks. I tried hard not to cry, but it was no use. I looked over to the wall where there were photographs of Grandma Kam smiling as she held me as a baby. There was one photograph she'd said was her favorite: It was the three of us at the beach on my second birthday. I had loved seeing the donkeys, she'd told me.

The door opened and Wai Gong came in. He was wearing his coat and the red scarf I'd used to save his life yesterday.

"Morning, Lizzie. I'm in a rush. I marked a big x on the calendar, which must mean I've got an important job interview today. I'm heading to the warehouse to see about a position." He took the red-and-gold calendar down from the wall and showed me where he had put a big fat purple x with a marker. "Do you think I need an umbrella? I do, don't I?" He hooked the calendar back onto the silver nail poking out of the wall.

I nodded and used my pajama sleeve to wipe away the tear that had fallen down my cheek. Surely he didn't have a job interview on a Sunday? I was about to tell him the x might have been about me, that it was my birthday, but I didn't. I wasn't going to tell him something he should already know.

"See you later, then," he said. And with that, he left. I wondered if I should keep a closer eye on him because of yesterday's incidents with the bus and the keys, but I just didn't have the energy to confront him, especially not on my birthday.

I sat on the edge of the sofa and took a deep breath. A photo of Grandma Kam and me laughing caught my attention. She used to say, "You've got to make the best out of a bad situation! Keep dancing through life, Lizzie!" She had lots of little sayings like that. I sat up straighter. She wouldn't want me moping around here feeling sorry for myself. I still had two brilliant friends. *It's not the end of the world*, I thought. I picked up my phone and texted Chi and Tyler.

ME

Hey you two!

CHI

Happy birthday! What's happening? We didn't get invited round this year. You okay?

28

TYLER

Yeah, your gramps didn't ask us over.

ME

Wai Gong forgot my birthday :o(

CHI

No way! Sorry Lizzie. Come to my house.

ME

No. I'm okay honestly.

CHI

It wasn't a question! Quit being home alone like in that film!

ME

All right.

CHI

Good. Tyler you come too.

TYLER

I can come later. Can I bring Bishop?

No clingy dogs today please, Tyler! And we can chat about Comic Con!

All right, but he's not going to be happy.

He's a dog!

Dogs have feelings too :0(

No Bishop!

See you!

I was so glad I could get out of the flat and go to Chi's and have a birthday celebration, even if it wasn't planned. No one really wants to be alone on their birthday, do they? Spending the day with my besties was good. The three of us had been close since nursery school. Chi had saved a small Tyler from

Marcus Bradbury, who had tried to stuff Tyler into the recycling bin because he said having two dads was "weird." Chi had told Marcus Bradbury to mind his own business, and I thought having two dads was way better than having no dads, like me. Tyler had been part of our crew ever since.

I put on my raincoat and ran down to Chi's house; she lived on the other side of Dumbarton Road in a terraced house. It usually only took me ten minutes, but I was extra speedy today because it was raining. I rang the bell and her mum, Jane, let me in. I carefully took off my soggy sneakers and put them in the shoe rack. They had white guest slippers for me to put on.

"Hi, Lizzie, come in. Happy birthday! Chi told us you were coming over. I'm glad I'm here—we've just hired a couple of new people at the café, so I'm getting more time off," Jane said, standing tall with her dark brown hair tied back in a scarlet scrunchie. She had opened a new Asian fusion vegan café a couple of years ago on Byres Road. Jane took my coat and hung it up in the small closet under the stairs.

I stood by the door to the living room, which was slightly open. I couldn't help but peer in. I could see sticks of nag champa incense burning on the coffee table, which had been pushed to the side of the room. It smelled different from the joss sticks Wai Gong burned while praying to his gods.

Chi's dad (he was called Cuong, but he wanted everyone to call him Tay instead) was doing a headstand on his mat in the middle of the carpet. His eyes were shut in concentration, his tie-dye T-shirt scrunched up around his shoulders, his six-pack on display. Tay was an ex-gymnast who had worked for Cirque Du Soleil in Las Vegas before he had kids with Jane. I couldn't remember the last time I'd even left Glasgow, never mind getting on a plane and going somewhere fancy like Las Vegas.

Jane came over and put her arm around my shoulders.

"He's nearly done," she said.

When I looked back into the living room, Tay was carefully putting his feet onto the floor one at a time. He stood upright and smiled at me. "Happy twelve times around the sun, Lizzie! Do you want me to cleanse your aura or give you some reiki so you can start your year feeling balanced and positive?"

"Erm, no thanks," I told him. I folded my arms, wondering if Chi's dad could tell I was feeling a little wobbly today and that was why he was offering me free energy healing. "I'm totally fine. But thanks for the offer!"

Jane called up the stairs, "Chi! Lizzie is here!" She sniffed the air. "Oh god! I'm burning the rice!" she said, running into the kitchen.

Minh, Chi's older brother, appeared on the stairs, his arms laden with filming equipment. He trudged down and put his stuff next to the door. He had floppy black hair and a crooked

32

smile that reminded me of V from BTS. I edged my way down the hallway to make room for him.

"Minh, I thought you were at the café helping Kai. He can't take the orders *and* cook the food," Jane said. "Annick doesn't start her shift until two."

"I was there, but it wasn't busy. He'll text me if it gets too busy for him. I was hoping to speak to you about me working every single weekend. A friend has asked me to film them singing for an audition tape," Minh said. "It's not fair, Mum."

I felt like I was intruding on some Pham family business.

"You asked for the job so you could earn some money to buy yourself a secondhand car and all that filming stuff, and *now* you want to quit?" Jane said.

Tay ushered me toward the stairs. I watched as Jane and Minh went to the living room for a mother-and-son talk.

"I just need to make a short documentary about . . . I dunno, about something, I haven't decided yet," Minh said, but then the door closed and his voice became muffled.

Tay shrugged. "They're more alike than they care to think. Families, eh?" Yes, families could be very tricky things indeed.

"Hey, Lizzie, I hope your grandfather is well. He could come over too if you want to invite him. I haven't seen him about much lately. Do you want to call him?" Tay asked.

"Oh, thanks, but he's gone out today," I said.

"We'd love for you to stay for lunch—Jane is trying out a new marinated tofu and eggplant dish with dates," Tay said.

"Oh, I'd love to stay for lunch . . . if you don't mind having me," I answered, but I was thinking about stuffing my face with party food instead: potato chips, jumbo sausage rolls, pizza. Weren't dates sweet? Would they go with tofu? But I didn't want to be rude. I didn't want to tell him that Chi was definitely *not* vegan when she came over to my house or that she was keeping a certain fast-food restaurant in business with her secret bacon double cheeseburger consumption.

"Of course. You can come here anytime, you know, especially if you need some time away," Tay said. "I was thinking we could do some family yoga if you're up for it this evening?" He grinned. "You can stand on my back and pretend I'm a paddleboard!" He laughed; small creases lined his eyes, which were the only clue that this man was in his forties. He had youthful Asian skin—you gotta love it! I hoped I looked like I was in my twenties when I was his age.

"It's her birthday, leave her alone!" I heard Chi shout from upstairs. "Sorry, Dad, no family yoga today!" Chi came padding down the stairs in a giraffe onesie. She grabbed my arm and pulled me up with her.

"Okay, but I'll make Lizzie a special dessert for her birthday, leave it to me!" Tay yelled up as Jane came out of the living room. I cringed at the thought. Chi made a vomit face behind her dad's back.

"Come upstairs, birthday star, I got you a cool present," said Chi. I followed her up to her room.

"I'm glad *someone* remembered my birthday," I said, plonking myself in the mushy comfort of her furry brown beanbag that resembled Chewbacca.

"Your gramps not remembering is strange. Your grandparents always made such a big deal about your birthday," she mused, sitting on her bed.

"I know. But it's been a hard year. He's not himself, but that's normal, right? When you lose someone you love?"

"Yes, I guess," she said.

"Maybe I shouldn't feel so bad about it," I said. "It's just a forgotten birthday. There are worse things going on in the world, right? Climate change, hunger, war, the refugee crisis, racism, famine. Me not getting a birthday cake or presents from my grandad isn't that bad. It's all relative, isn't it?"

"God, Lizzie! You are the worst twelve-year-old in the history of the world. Of course you deserve cake and presents! You need to start enjoying yourself more. I've noticed how sad you've been looking lately. I hope this helps. Open it!" She handed me a red box with a bow on it.

I lifted the lid, and inside was a green journal covered in gold leaves, some gel pens, and a little Jabba the Hutt stress toy. I laughed. Chi couldn't help herself. She always had to get me something from *Star Wars*.

"Thanks, Chi," I said. "What's this?" I held up a pink stone.

"Oh, my dad put that in there—it's rose quartz for your heart chakra, he said. But my gift is way cooler. You can squeeze that Jabba when you feel down. I know looking after the house like you do is a drag," Chi said.

"It's a really thoughtful present," I said, giving her a big hug.

"I'm glad Tyler is coming over," Chi said. "I want to talk to him about Comic Con and my costume. I'm going as Princess Leia from *Star Wars*, with the iconic hair buns." Chi got up and took a hanger with a shiny white hooded robe from the back of her bedroom door. "What do you think? Tyler's dad helped him get the hood part right. It's a bit long, I think. I might ask Tyler to take the hem up a little this week." She held it over the bed, and I stroked the soft satin material.

"It's great, Chi, you'll look amazing. It is a bit long though, you're right."

"Thanks! I'm so excited about going. Minh's not excited about taking us, but he can get over himself. Mum just wants him to get us there—we can do what we want once we're inside. She's always worried about me. I keep telling her I'm twelve and can go places by myself. I mean, you do the shopping all by your-self, don't you?" Chi asked.

"I do," I said.

"Are you excited about Comic Con?" she asked.

The answer was both "yes" and "I'm not sure." Of course, I was buzzing to spend the whole day seeing people dressed up as their favorite comic and anime characters all under one roof, and the thing I was most pumped about was seeing some of my favorite actors on panels. And I was definitely happy to be going because it was something different from my usual boring routine of shopping and chores. I'd been saving my money for months for the ticket, and Tyler was still trying to convince me that I should dress up too, but I was a little terrified. What if I looked silly or people laughed at me? I usually wore black jeans and a T-shirt. I didn't like to stand out.

A boy named Dylan in our grade had once said I had "legs like a man." Chi had put him in his place. Tyler said people just say things because they want to get a reaction from you or to look funny in front of their friends. He said he'd learned not to let it get to him. He was proud to have two loving dads, and no one really said anything about that anymore.

Luke had once called me "Old Lady Lizzie" at school because he'd seen me with my gran's old tartan shopping cart. I didn't use it again after that. But I'd done what Tyler said and didn't let it get to me, and Luke had stopped saying it.

"Tyler's going with the Trekkies from school. We can pretend we are not best friends with him for one day. Please dress up with me! It's so much fun being someone else for a while. It's Comic Con: Trust me, you won't look strange at all. There are going to be loads of *out-there* costumes from all different franchises—*Star Wars*, Marvel, DC, loads of anime characters . . ."

"But what could I go as?" I asked. I was drawing a blank. The thought of being someone else for a while was appealing right now, but still, the idea of putting on a costume and walking around the convention center with people taking photos was very daunting.

Just then, the door to Chi's room opened and Tyler walked in, smiling like he'd won a prize.

"Hey, Lizster! Happy birthday to ya! Happy birthday to ya! Happy birthday!" Tyler sang the famous Stevie Wonder version of the song, dancing while pointing at me. He was wearing a very smart blue suit jacket. "This is very different from your granny's parties in your living room," he said. Chi glared at him.

"There's nothing wrong with having a wee party in *my* room. Lizzie's had a terrible morning. Her gramps forgetting her birthday is literally the worst," Chi said, rubbing my back.

"Yeah, I couldn't believe your message. *We* didn't forget though. Here!" Tyler held out his hands. In them was a hastily wrapped parcel covered in the *Glasgow Daily Times*.

"We didn't have gift wrap; it's artisanal wrapping paper, recycled and good for the planet," Tyler said.

"Thanks, I'm glad you could come."

I ripped the tape off the newspaper, and in the middle was a pair of fluffy green slippers with eyes on the front. They were kind of cute and funny, and when I put my hands in the feet bits, I felt something hard. I pulled out whatever it was. It was wrapped in the sports section. Tyler tilted his head in anticipation.

"I hope you like it. I thought you could do with a little sparkle in your life right now. I got it done at Braehead Shopping

Center—there's a kiosk there where you can get a photo turned into anything you want."

It was a snow globe the size of my fist, and inside was Wai Gong, Grandma Kam, and me. The photo was the one I used for my lock screen on my phone.

I shook it, and purple and silver glitter poured down over our faces. Grandma Kam was laughing. I shook it again and watched the slivers of light move in the water.

"Thanks, Ty, I love it." I gave him a hug.

"But you like my presents too, right?" Chi said, pouting. She tapped the journal and gel pens. "Mine's more practical. For recording your innermost thoughts. Or for writing about people you don't like at school!"

"I love them all," I said, shaking the snow globe and watching the glitter fall around our smiling faces.

CHAPTER FIVE

People Make Glasgow

"Come on down, you guys, lunch is ready!" Jane called.

I swapped the white slippers for the ones Tyler had bought me. They were soft and comfy. We all rushed downstairs.

We went into the kitchen, where the table had been covered in a paper tablecloth with rainbow spots on it. There were small white-and-blue bowls laid out with chopsticks resting on little china pillows on the side. Tay was holding out a silver baking tray with something brown and sticky on it.

"Tay made you a no-bake avocado and cacao pudding—all vegan!" said Jane. "And we have soy candles, so you will have a birthday cake after all!"

"Okay . . . well, I'm sure Lizzie doesn't want to be a guinea pig for your cake thing here," Chi said, making air quotes when she said the word *cake*. I literally couldn't help it—I had to laugh. I could always count on Chi to make me laugh. The motto of our city was People Make Glasgow. Today might not have been like the birthdays I'd had in the past, but everyone was trying their best to make my day memorable. And vegan sludge was certainly very memorable!

"Oh, wow," said Tyler, "this is definitely a birthday like no other." He nudged me in the ribs, and I chuckled again.

We sat down at the table, and Chi kept looking at me and mouthing, "I'm sorry." I laughed. Tyler sat down but put his hands over his bowl when offered food.

"Oh no, none for me, thanks, Mr. Pham. I already ate my lunch before I came. I'm so full now. But thanks!" Tyler grinned a very innocent grin. His eyes told a different story as they darted around the table in amusement. "Bon appétit, Lizzie," Tyler said. He loved rubbing it in. "I wish I hadn't filled up already." He patted his belly.

"You can take some home with you in a container, Tyler," said Jane. "You look very fancy today."

"This ensemble . . ." He stroked the sleeve of his suit jacket. "I made it with my dad's help."

I looked at Tyler's suit and imagined myself in something similar. "It's gorgeous, Ty. I wish I could make myself something like that," I said. Tyler was brilliant at making his own clothes. It helped that one of his dads did that for a living—George had met loads of famous people in his job at the theater. Tyler was the most creative out of the three of us. Some of the boys in our class made fun of him for not liking football, but whenever it was no uniform day, Tyler always looked the best and the most original.

"Come on, kids, eat up or it'll get cold," Tay said, standing at the table and spooning rice into everyone's bowls.

I picked up a cube of marinated tofu and dropped it into my bowl. It didn't look *that* terrible. I scooped up some brown rice and added some salad but avoided the stewed dates. The rice was kind of nutty and chewier than the jasmine rice we ate at home, but it wasn't bad. The tofu just didn't taste of anything despite being marinated in soy sauce, ginger, and garlic.

Chi moaned about the food her mum served at home, but it beat having to scour the supermarkets for yellow sale labels on food about to expire. Or having your food used as an offering and deemed too sacred to eat. That had happened a couple of times recently; Wai Gong had given some of our food to his deities on the shelf in his bedroom, then said we couldn't eat it afterward.

I gobbled rice and tofu down as I realized how hungry I was. I looked around the table, happy that I wasn't alone on my birthday. I wondered what Wai Gong was doing. I hoped he was okay.

"So did you get anything nice for your birthday?" Jane asked.

"Erm, Mum, leave it, okay? She doesn't want to talk about that," Chi said. I wished she wouldn't speak for me.

"It's okay, I'm fine," I said. "Well, my grandad didn't get me anything. In fact, he forgot about my birthday completely.

I guess he's got a lot on his mind. But I got lovely presents from Chi and Tyler." I filled my mouth with a spongy cube of fried tofu, then another so that I didn't have to speak. I chomped slowly.

"That doesn't sound like your grandad," said Tay, looking puzzled.

"Sounds really difficult, Lizzie. Do you want me to come and talk to him?" asked Jane. "I don't see him much these days. It must be hard now that it's just the two of you. Let me know if you need some help, okay?"

"We're fine. He's got his interests and I've got mine," I told her. It was hard enough telling Chi what was going on.

"You know you can always rely on us to help, Lizzie," Tyler said. Tay patted him on the back and started cleaning up the bowls.

"Tyler's always thinking about others, isn't that right, Tyler?" said Tay. "Chi, you could be more like that, you know—a bit more community minded."

Minh laughed and almost spit out his rice.

"What's so funny, big head?" said Chi. "I help . . . some people . . . sometimes. Don't I, Lizzie?"

I nodded. Chi did help me in her own way. When she wasn't thinking about herself first, she could be nice to people.

"Yeah, right," said Minh. "When Bà Nội came from Hanoi to visit, you wouldn't even give her your bedroom. She stayed in my room, and I slept on the couch."

"That's only because your bed is harder and I thought she would like it more than mine," said Chi, looking a little put out.

I stood up and began to take some of the bowls to the counter next to the sink.

"Sit down, Lizzie," Tay said. "It's your birthday, you don't need to clear up." It was a habit, I guess. Tidying up after eating was second nature now. I felt bad seeing someone else take the bowls away. I'd gotten used to being the one to do that kind of stuff.

"Do you think you need help at home?" Jane continued, turning the conversation back to me. I felt my cheeks get hot as everyone looked at me.

"My aunt is a social worker—she might be able to help you," Tyler said.

I shook my head, uncomfortable. "No, no . . . we're fine . . . I'm fine," I said. I didn't want social workers to get involved, or Chi's parents. Things were okay. We were getting along without anyone's help.

"Lizzie is excited about going to Comic Con for the first time, aren't you?" Chi said. I nodded. I was glad she had changed the subject.

"Do you like all that superhero and intergalactic *Star Wars* stuff too, Lizzie?" Tay asked. "We were hoping our kids would grow out of it, but they seem to have gone the opposite way. Minh has been making some spoof short films. 'May the force be with you' and all that." Tay laughed. Minh didn't look up and continued to shovel more food into his mouth.

"So . . . shall we do the candles now?" Jane said. She held up the "cake." Tay got out a lighter and lit twelve candles in the middle of the weird healthy vegan gloop. The candles burned bright at first but then started to wobble while they all sang "Happy Birthday." Minh took out his phone and began filming, moving around the room to make sure everyone was included.

"Happy birthday to you! Make a wish!" Chi said. "If you don't, then I will!"

I wished for Wai Gong to be okay. I wished I could make him happy again. I wished he could dance the cha-cha again like he wanted. That was all.

I blew as hard as I could before the candles fell over, but I accidentally made some gloop splash onto Jane's face as she held the tray, and she dropped it. From that moment on, it was like a slow-motion film—everyone held out their hands, trying to stop the baking tray from hitting the floor. The candles toppled over like dominoes, and the brown gloopy no-bake avocado "cake" splattered on everyone's clothes as Tay caught it in one wobbly palm, his legs sliding into a half split.

I was speechless. It was quite the show. I clapped my hands. Then I used my index finger to gather some of the gloop from my top and tasted it.

"Yum . . . oh, it's okay, actually. Too bad there's not a lot left," I said with fake concern.

"You have what's left, Lizzie," Tay said, handing me a spoon and the half-empty tray. "It's your birthday, after all."

Tyler started to giggle, and then I did, and then no one could help themself. We'd all caught the giggles. We had to hold our bellies. It was just what I needed.

CHAPTER SIX

An Unexpected Gift

When I got home after my eventful and impromptu birthday at the Phams', Wai Gong was standing outside our front door muttering to himself. He was wearing his inside slippers. What was going on? Then I saw what he was holding. He was cradling his Guan Yin statue, but it was in two pieces. I gasped when I saw it.

"What happened? Didn't you get the job?" I asked, rushing over.

"No, I made a mistake. The interview wasn't today."

"Are you okay? You look pale."

Wai Gong's hands were trembling. "I knocked her over when I was looking for this." He handed me a green envelope. I looked at the front, confused. Large gold letters read: TO LIZZIE.

He put the goddess's body under his arm and held the head and shoulder part up in front of him. "I'm *so* sorry, Goddess. I didn't mean to break you in half!" Wai Gong was shivering. He didn't even have his red scarf on.

"Come on, let's get inside and we can sort this all out." I ushered him in and shut the door with my hip. The flat was nearly as cold as it was outside. "Let's put the heat on, Wai Gong. You can't sit inside freezing." I put down the envelope and my gifts from Chi and Tyler. We put on our slippers, and as I passed the thermostat, I turned on the heat.

"Lizzie, I remembered why I had an *x* on the calendar! I was supposed to give you this card on your birthday. It is your birthday today, isn't it?" He placed the bottom of the statue on the hall table and tried to attach the top part, matching up the shoulders with the rest of the body, but it toppled off. Wai Gong seemed distressed. "But then once I remembered, I forgot where I'd put it. I came home and I searched and searched. I looked high and low. I almost gave up until I saw it under the goddess. I had put it there for safekeeping, only I knocked her to the floor when I pulled the envelope out. I'm such a clumsy guy. Now my luck is truly bad." He paused. "But I'm glad I found this for you. I suppose that is a good thing."

I nodded. I was trying to find words, but nothing would come. I could see Wai Gong was conflicted; he'd broken his favorite goddess statue but had remembered that it was my birthday. I felt odd too—I was happy that he'd finally thought about me, and there was a bit of me that was also secretly glad the goddess was broken. He never talked to me the way he talked to that ornament.

"It's from Kam . . . she told me not to forget. But I did. Sorry that I'm not clever like your grandma, Lizzie." His hands were shaking. "I've let you down. We didn't have a party. I forgot to decorate with balloons, and I forgot to hide presents . . . I'm terrible." He looked forlorn.

"Oh, Wai Gong, no. You're being too harsh on yourself. I thought you had forgotten my birthday, and here you are with a present from Gran. I'm glad you finally remembered about the card. Thank you," I said, and gave him a tight hug. "Don't worry about the balloons and all that stuff. I've had a fun day at Chi's place."

"But I should have been with you today, Lizzie," he said. "I walked along the canals and thought I'd check out the charity shops on the way home, but most of them were closed."

"I know you feel bad about it, but please don't. Let's see what she got me. I'm so excited."

I slowly ripped the envelope flap and pulled out a birthday card and a gold chain with a circular jade pendant. Inside the card were four tickets with a tower logo on them. They were gold with black trim around the edges.

"This is so amazing!" I passed them to Wai Gong so I could read the card.

"Ahhh, tickets to the Blackpool Tower Ballroom for Sunday, November eighteenth!" Wai Gong exclaimed.

"Oh, wow," I said. I couldn't wait to read what she had written to me. I sat on an arm of the sofa. I instantly recognized Grandma Kam's handwriting, and a lump formed in my throat. Her cursive script was spindly but quite beautiful. It read:

Dear Lizzie,

Happy twelfth birthday, my dearest. I wish I could be there to celebrate with you. I'm really sorry that I'm not around. I hope your wai gong is looking after you well and that you are looking after each other.

I'm so sorry I didn't have time to teach you the cha-cha—I would have loved to have spent more time with you. I bought you tickets for afternoon tea at the Blackpool Tower Ballroom, and you can take yer wee pals too. As you know, that is where I met your grandfather. It's making me teary thinking about you both there without me. I treasured our family nights at home watching Strictly together.

Look after the old-timer—you're all each other has now. If your grandad is right, then I'm floating around with his favorite goddess up in some celestial realm. I hope you both enjoy the magic and KEEP DANCING!

I love you!

Granny Kam

I began crying like I hadn't cried in a long time. Wai Gong rushed over and put his arms around me.

"Why are you crying, Lizzie? Are you sad about the gift? It's not what you wanted?"

"Oh no, I love it! They're happy tears! She wants us to dance and to remember her. It's the best gift."

"The Mecca of ballroom dancing. It's just like Kam to think of such a wonderful gift. I miss her so much," he said. "I wish I could dance the cha-cha with her one last time."

Wai Gong looked over at the photo of Grandma Kam on the wall of memory I had created when she had passed away. He gulped. I could see he was trying not to cry like me. But then he couldn't help it, and we laughed and cried together.

I held the tickets and the necklace in my hands and looked at a photo of Grandma Kam on the wall. She was smiling. I felt this was a sign that she was looking out for us from wherever she was, just like the peacock in the Guan Yin story.

CHAPTER SEVEN

Old Lady Lizzie

The next day, I rushed over to Chi in class, as I wanted to tell her the great news about the four tickets to Blackpool that Grandma Kam had left as her parting gift. Minh had dropped her off on his way to college, so she was already at her desk when I arrived.

"Hey, guess what?" I said, sliding into my chair beside her.

"You were abducted by aliens, but they brought you back because you were needed on Earth?" she said while checking her face in her phone's camera. I started to tell her about what happened when I arrived home. But Chi began holding her hair up in a ponytail. "Do I look more like Rey from *The Force Awakens* or Princess Leia? Tyler said I look Rey-ish. But Leia's my number one hero; she's so classy, right?"

I wondered if she had heard anything I had said. She was too much sometimes.

"Rey? And no, there were no aliens. When I got home last night, Wai Gong *did* have a present for me. Two presents, actually! Only they weren't from him. They were from Grandma Kam!"

Tyler came over and sat on my desk.

"But how is that possible? She's . . . you know," he said awkwardly.

"Dead?" Chi added, tactless as usual. "My dad says we should talk more about death because it's going to happen to all of us one day. The Buddhists talk about it all the time, he says."

"I was going to say *no longer with us*," Tyler said. "Or *in heaven*. But yes, she has passed away. So how did she get you a present?"

"Well, Grandma Kam gave Wai Gong an envelope to keep for me until my birthday! I think that's why he's been acting all strange," I told them. "He was looking for it and didn't want me to know he'd lost it. It sort of explains things."

"Wow, that's cool, Lizzie," Chi said. She stopped admiring herself.

"He'd put an *x* on the calendar to remind him, but he'd forgotten why he'd put it there. Anyway . . . to make a long story short, we've got tickets to the Blackpool Tower Afternoon Tea Experience for all four of us! It's where Grandma Kam and Wai Gong used to dance when they were younger. We've not been on holiday or even on a day trip for years. I'm so excited to leave Glasgow and get away from the horizontal rain! Wai Gong didn't even know that was the present. He was as surprised as I was! And she got me this too." I pulled out the jade pendant from under my shirt and showed Chi and Tyler.

"Oh my god, Lizzie. That is a brilliant birthday present," Chi said. "A day trip to Blackpool is going to be mega. You know they have the Pleasure Beach part with all those rides. They have a massive roller coaster too. I can't wait!"

"Ahh, that sounds so amazing! Roller coasters, eating fish and chips by the sea! It was so sweet of her to let Chi and me come too," Tyler said. "I've never actually been to the seaside, you know."

"No way," I said, pretending I was more well traveled than I really was. When Grandma Kam was alive, we'd sometimes get the bus to Largs or the train to Troon.

"You've never seen the sea, seriously?" Chi said. "It's not that far away, you know."

"I know! But we always go to London or to my nan's bungalow in Manchester when we have school holidays. We did go to Italy that one time when Pops was attending a conference at the University of Milan. Dad and I spent some time sightseeing, but we were far away from the sea. I've seen the sea from a plane though!"

"That's not the same as standing on a beach and looking out at the horizon," Chi said.

"I've never been abroad. You're so lucky, Ty. I hope we can make this day trip happen," I said.

"I'm glad your gramps didn't forget you after all you do for him. We don't see you enough because you're always doing boring stuff," Chi said. She was being a little harsh; she didn't seem to realize that I *had* to do all that "boring stuff." Unlike in her family, there was nobody else to help us, and we didn't have money from two businesses like the Phams did.

"Grandma Kam wanted us to be happy after she'd gone—it feels like we've been given another chance to be a family again. This is going to be so good for Wai Gong!"

"Hey, you know what would be really fun?" Chi said. "What if you learned your grandma's favorite dance and danced with your grandad at the Blackpool Tower Ballroom? That would blow his mind."

"That's a great idea! My grandma was going to teach me the cha-cha because we loved that dance the most when we watched *Strictly*. But then she got ill and she didn't get the chance. What do you think, Ty?"

Tyler nodded. "I love it! You've got to do it! We know you don't like being the center of attention, but your grandma sent this gift to you from her deathbed. It's her final wish."

The thought of learning to dance made me feel a little sick, but Tyler was right. It was my opportunity to have fun and make Wai Gong happy at the same time. Plus, no one knew me in Blackpool, so even if I was terrible, who would care?

"There's one massive problem though, isn't there?" I realized. "Where am I going to get the money for dance lessons?"

"Check out that place near Byres Road—it's down that lane by the vintage clothes shop. They're probably not that expensive," Chi said. Chi had no idea how much things really cost.

"Or you can learn from YouTube," Tyler said. "That's where I get a lot of ideas for costumes and outfits." I knew I could rely on Tyler to be the voice of reason. He knew that Chi sometimes forgot about what things were like in the real world.

"Yeah, that's a good idea, Ty. My cousin Tuyen learned how to play the piano from YouTube," said Chi. "And Minh learned loads of his filmmaking stuff from watching videos online. I'm sure you can find ones to help you, Lizzie."

"Speaking of money, how are we actually going to get to Blackpool?" Tyler asked. "I've only got twenty pounds, and I don't think that will be enough for train tickets for us all. I don't think I can ask for any more money this month, since my dad gave me money for my *Star Trek* outfit."

In all my excitement about having the tickets to Blackpool Tower, I hadn't thought about the practicalities. We didn't have a car, and neither did Tyler's dads. It was a long train journey; I wasn't sure how Wai Gong would manage, as he wasn't good at sitting for a long time. The Phams were busy on weekends with their businesses, so they wouldn't be able to take us.

Any spare money I did have had gone to my Comic Con ticket. There was no magic money tree where I could pluck off leaves of cash for dance lessons and travel to Blackpool. How was I ever going to get everyone there?

Mrs. Begum came in to take attendance, and the chatter began to lessen. Tyler went to his seat behind us.

"Now, everyone, parents' evening is this Thursday. Your parents should have booked via the online booking system. I am open to bribes of Tunnock's tea cakes and toffee apples, should you want a more glowing review of your schoolwork." Mrs. Begum was funny.

"Miss, why is it called parents' evening?" Annie asked. "I live with my uncle and his girlfriend now until my dad gets out of the army."

Tyler said, "My auntie works for social services, and lots of kids don't live with their parents. They should change the name of it." Tyler was the opposite of Chi in many ways, not only the *Star Trek* vs. *Star Wars* thing. He was also always looking for a worthy cause to get involved with.

"Yeah. Some people in this class don't have parents," said Hannah.

"Like Old Lady Lizzie," jeered Luke. I thought that *old lady* thing had been put to rest already. I wanted the earth to swallow me. I didn't turn around to look at him. I just remained still and pretended I hadn't heard.

"She's not an old lady, and don't you talk about her like that," Chi said, sticking up for me.

I was always being made to feel like I didn't quite belong or teased because I didn't have enough money to buy the stuff the rest of my classmates had. A few months ago, Kiera McAllister had made fun of me because I always wore trousers, unlike the rest of the girls. Then, a few weeks ago, she'd made comments about my hair being uneven because I'd cut it myself. I remembered what Tyler had said and tried not to let it get to me. Luke was always picking on me. Sometimes he said that because I lived with old people, I smelled of mothballs. The worst thing was when he started to mock Chinese accents. He kept shouting "flied lice" across the playground. Tyler said I should tell Mrs. Begum, but I didn't. Chi was fuming, and I don't know what she said to him, but he stopped saying racist things after that.

"Okay, that's enough, everyone," said Mrs. Begum. "We don't call people names. We do not talk about other people's family members. Luke, just because someone looks and acts different from what you're used to doesn't mean that they are strange." Mrs. Begum appeared flustered. "And Annie and Tyler, that's a good point about parents' evening, and I apologize. You are right—some people live with other guardians or carers. Thank you for bringing that up."

Mrs. Begum sat down and rattled off names for attendance before saying, "Right, class, open your books to page one hundred and five. *The orphans had escaped . . .*"

I sat in my chair, blocking out the sound of Mrs. Begum droning on about an old book with more orphans; it was making me feel glum. Not everyone without parents had to be street thieves or dirty or whatever. Wai Gong had always been a parent to me, and now I was determined to help him. I was going to take him to Blackpool and fulfill Grandma Kam's dream. I knew Wai Gong would love it too. If I could get him there, it would help him get over Grandma Kam and back to his old self.

CHAPTER EIGHT

Step by Step

On Thursday after school, I walked to the dance studio Chi had mentioned, Step by Step, which was down one of the lanes off Byres Road. I wanted to see if they had a discount for kids. Maybe it wouldn't be that expensive and I could buy a couple of lessons for myself.

I went in, and a stern-looking lady with brown hair tied back very tightly came over. She looked me up and down.

"Can I help you?" She sounded posh; she wasn't from Glasgow. She sounded like Prue from *The Great British Bake Off*.

"Yes, I hope you can. I was wondering about Latin dance lessons, specifically the cha-cha." I stood tall to show her how serious I was about it.

"For you?" She said it like I was a fly in her soup. "I'm afraid not. All of our children's lessons are fully booked, and the waiting list is rather long."

My shoulders slumped. "How much are adult lessons, then? Couldn't I just come to a couple of adult lessons? I just want to pick up the basics. It's for a special occasion," I told her. My palms were sweating, so I wiped them on my trousers.

"They're fifteen pounds an hour. I'm sorry, I just can't help you." She started to move forward, so I backed up, and I was at the door when she said, "If it's for losing weight, you could jog around the botanic garden for free." Then she shut the door in my face and walked back into her silly dance studio.

I stood there for a minute or two, rooted to the spot. I was so angry, I let out a massive yell. "ARGHHHHH!" I wasn't going to let some evil Maleficent-looking witch tell me that I couldn't learn to dance! I was going to learn from YouTube like Tyler had suggested. It was free, and I would show that woman just what Lizzie Chu could do!

When I got home, the communal front door was open. Mrs. McGuigan was on her hands and knees, scrubbing the steps. I saw that she'd pulled the weeds out from the side.

"Hi, Lizzie," she said. "These dandelions are a nuisance. I've been pulling them out for half an hour now."

"You're doing a great job, Mrs. M," I told her.

"Do you want to lend a hand?" she asked.

"Oh, I can't right now. I'm expecting a couple of friends soon. Can you tell them I'll leave the door ajar for them and to come in?" I asked her. "One's called Tyler, and the other is Chi—just ask them for their names."

"Sure thing, hen," she said, dipping her hands into her bucket of soapy water. She was like the neighborhood watch.

I ran up the stairs, kicked my sneakers off, and ran to my room. Tyler and Chi were going to come over soon to show me their Comic Con outfits. But before they got here, I wanted to practice dancing. I shut my door and grabbed my phone. I found a video of two dance teachers from New York demonstrating what they called "the cha-cha basics." I propped it up on my dresser and got ready.

The man was called Brian—he was in his thirties and dressed in grey sweatpants and a white T-shirt. The woman, Nancy, wore a black leotard and shiny leggings. They both looked kinder than the woman at Step by Step, that was for sure.

The instructions sounded easy. I replayed the beginning of the clip.

"Forward, forward, forward, walk, walk, walk, then back, back, back . . ." Brian said, his perfect, straight white teeth sparkling like those in toothpaste ads. I swiped back and followed Brian's instructions. What was it again? Forward,

forward, back, back? It looked easy when Brian and Nancy did it.

He mentioned "Cuban action in the hip area." I tried to move my hips from side to side like they did on *Strictly*, but I looked like an ironing board being unfolded. Then he mentioned being on the "balls of your feet." I lifted my right foot and looked for anything that resembled a sphere. Nope, couldn't see any ball-like things on my feet. I didn't get what he was talking about.

Just then, the door to my bedroom opened and Tyler came in. I felt embarrassed and quickly dropped my foot to the floor.

"Don't mind me," Tyler said. "Are you trying to do the standing splits or balance on one leg like a flamingo?"

I could feel my face getting hot.

"Ha ha, you're funny. No, I thought I had a splinter in my foot, but it's okay now." I didn't want to mention that I was searching for the balls of my feet just in case it was something everyone knew about and I was being dense.

"Oh, you're doing your cha-cha dance thingy, aren't you? Carry on," Tyler said. He glanced at my phone. Brian from New York was doing something complicated now. "What's that guy saying—*side together*?"

"Oh, that's nothing." I wanted desperately to change the subject; I didn't think this dancing thing was going to work out. "Did you bring over your sewing stuff?" I picked up my phone and tapped Brian and Nancy off the screen. I'd come back to it when I was alone.

"Come on, Lizzie, it's me. You know I'm your biggest fan. What is that?"

"All right, it's a cha-cha basics video. Do you remember telling me I could learn anything from YouTube?"

Tyler nodded.

"Well, I tried, but it's not feeling right. I can't do it. It looks easy, but when I do it, I'm terrible."

"Ah, you just need to keep doing it—fake it till you make it!" Tyler said. "It's practice, isn't it? It's like sewing. I've been getting better at it because I've made mistakes and practiced. The first pair of trousers I made had one leg longer than the other." He chuckled.

"I dunno, maybe it was a silly idea," I said.

"You can do it, Lizzie. You've got weeks to learn the basics. I'm sure you can pick it up. Let me know if you need a partner or something. Or just a cheerleader."

"Thanks, Ty."

We both heard Chi arrive.

"Princess Leia is in the house!" she said, dropping two large bags on the floor. "What's going on in here?"

Tyler and I looked at each other.

"What are you two talking about?" Chi asked.

I looked at Tyler and shook my head. I didn't want Chi to know that I was failing at dance. Everything came easily to her.

Chi stood on top of my footstool in a grey tank top and leggings. Tyler handed her the white robe, which she slid over her head.

"I was telling Lizzie all about my latex Spock ears and how they make my ears sweat." Chi pulled a face, and we knew that was the end of that conversation. Whenever Tyler brought up anything from his favorite show, Chi switched off.

"This robe is too long—can you take it up a bit?" Chi asked. Tyler nodded and started to pin the bottom.

"Satin isn't the easiest material to work with," Tyler muttered to himself—carefully, as he had four pins poking out of his mouth. "When I go to fashion college, I am never going to work with satin ever again. I'm a crushed velvet kinda guy. I'll hand sew this here and then I can machine sew it when I get home."

Chi was humming the *Star Wars* theme. I began to join in, but then Tyler began humming the *Star Trek* theme in retaliation, but his singing was much worse, as he still had a couple of pins in his mouth. He started to pin the fabric tighter around Chi's body.

"Ouch! Be careful, Ty. I don't want to get blood on it before Saturday," Chi said.

"Sorry!" His fingers were shaking a little. If anyone ruined Chi's *looks*, as she called them, they would never hear the last of it.

My mind went back to Tyler's smart blue suit jacket. I wished I had an outfit like that but with a bow tie.

"I like your jacket, Ty," I said, admiring the lapels and the neatly sewn-on buttons. "The other day I read an article about a girl who went to her prom dressed in a tuxedo. They're so cool." I just wasn't into dresses. I didn't care what Kiera McAllister said.

"Are your parents going to the parents' and guardians' evening tonight?" I asked them.

"Yeah, mine booked ages ago," Chi said. Tyler nodded, the pins hanging out of his lips making him look like a vampire.

"Wai Gong didn't book, and he didn't go to the last one either. The school sent a letter home with me today, and I opened it." I dug it out of my schoolbag. "I haven't shown it to Wai Gong yet, as I don't want him to get worried or confused." I chewed on my bottom lip and handed it to Chi.

Dear Mr. Chu,

I hope this letter finds you well. We realized you hadn't booked a spot for a parent/guardian consultation. We are concerned that we haven't had any contact with you for some time now regarding Lizzie's learning journey.

Lizzie is doing well, although her teacher Mrs. Begum has noticed she often looks tired during attendance, and her other teachers have mentioned Lizzie failing to hand in homework.

Do let us know if there is anything our school community can do to assist you and Lizzie. We have an excellent pastoral care officer called Andrea Harris, and we would be happy to put you in touch with her. Her number is at the top of the letter, should you wish to discuss anything further.

Yours sincerely,
Mrs. Tabitha Arnold
Head Teacher

"I'm worried," I told them.

Chi read the letter. She passed it to Tyler, who shook his head.

"There's nothing to be worried about. I'm sure everyone who doesn't sign up for parents' evening gets one of these letters. I'd get him to call the office and say he's busy. Then the school will be satisfied that everything is fine," Tyler said.

I wanted to ask if they thought I should say something at school about why I didn't hand in my homework sometimes. But Chi started to yelp.

"Oww! You stabbed me! Watch it!" She scowled at Tyler.

"Relax, Chi, it was just a little nick," said Tyler. He sat back on his haunches and looked up at Chi, admiring his handiwork. I had to admit she looked good. He held up a mirror for her, and she twirled. Suddenly, Chi Naomi Pham had disappeared, and in her place was a convincing Princess Leia. My little drama was put on the back burner. I folded the letter from school and shoved it into my pocket.

"I look great, don't I?" Chi said, admiring herself in the mirror.

"You really do," I said, a little envious. I bet if Chi had shown up at Step by Step, that lady wouldn't have treated her the same way.

"I can make you a simple costume too, Lizzie. I could do it tomorrow night," Tyler said, a hopeful look on his face.

"No, it's totally okay. I'm fine not dressing up," I told him. Comic Con was two days away and both of my friends were still trying to get me into a costume!

"There's going to be an awesome Asian actors panel that we have to go to!" Chi said. "There'll be actors from *Doctor Strange* and *Shang-Chi*, and that X-wing pilot Captain Carson Teva is going to be there. I've got to get as many autographs as I can. I can't wait!"

"No way," I said. Chi and I had watched Marvel's *Shang-Chi* about fifty times already. Loads of people in our class made fun of Chi when the film came out because it had *Chi* in the title. People could be so silly and ignorant!

I helped Chi out of her Princess Leia outfit and hung it up on the back of my door.

"See you, Mr. Sewing Man and Princess Leia!" I said, waving as they went out.

"Later, Lizster!" Tyler shouted back.

Chi bent down and did that thing from the first *Star Wars* film.

"Help me, Obi-Wan Kenobi," she said. Then she grinned. "You're our only hope . . . oh, oh! You know what would be funny?"

"I know what you are going to say, and the answer is a big fat no. I definitely will not be dressing up as R2-D2 so you can do that line from the film!"

"Lizzie, you can read my mind! You sure I can't convince you?" She laughed.

"Nope! Now go home!" I said.

"See you tomorrow," Chi said. "And don't worry about the letter from school."

"Bye," I said, shutting the door behind her.

I pulled out the crumpled letter. Should I give it to Wai Gong? It would only upset him, I thought. I put it into the recycling bin in the kitchen.

On my way back through the living room, I saw Wai Gong's broken Guan Yin statue on the table. Her head was sitting next to her body, still with its serene smile. I picked up Guan Yin's head and shoulders and tried to piece her back together.

"Why does he like you so much?" I asked the broken goddess. "Will he be all right? Not that you're even listening, are you, because you're just a statue."

I heard the front door open. Wai Gong had returned home. He came in wearing his shoes. We always took them off when we arrived home—what was going on?

"Shoes off, Wai Gong!" I said. He looked down and shook his head. "Ah-ya, why have I still got these things on?" He hopped around on one foot, trying to yank his right shoe off. Then banged his shoulder on the wall. "Oww!"

"Undo the laces!" I told him, my face scrunched up. It was painful to watch.

"Laces? Yes. Of course." He stood like a drunken flamingo, rocking from one side to the other. I thought he was going to fall on his face. I helped steady him so he could undo his laces. I could smell his sweaty feet.

"Here are your flip-flops," I said, kicking them in his direction. He put them on, stumbled into the living room, and plopped down into his armchair.

"What a day I've had. You wouldn't believe it. I was sure I would get a new job. But I walked into many shops, and no one would hire me. I asked one place if they wanted me to deliver their food, and they asked if I had a bike or a car. 'I've got two legs,' I told them. They told me to get out!"

"Oh no, I'm sorry to hear that, Wai Gong," I told him.

"Then I needed to sit down because my feet were hurting so much from all the trudging around. I sat down at a nice café and ordered a green tea. But when I had to pay for it, my wallet was gone. I lost it, Lizzie!"

"Oh no, don't worry. We can go look for it. Come on." I was about to open the living room door so we could go search for the wallet, but Wai Gong put his head in his hands. Then he looked up. He stared at the broken goddess on the living room table.

"It's all because of her," he said, pointing at the pieces of the Guan Yin statue. His finger was shaking. "I've got terrible luck because *she* is broken. It's a sign, Lizzie! I can't do anything right now . . . I just need to stay inside so I can't get into more trouble. I'm going to hide here for a while."

"I'm sure we can glue her back together. You don't have bad luck; it's just that sometimes things happen that you can't control."

"No, you don't understand. I'm not going out again. I'm staying at home from now on! I certainly can't go to Blackpool either. The goddess breaking in half is an omen. My mind is made up. I've been adding it all up, and the Blackpool tickets are the reason Guan Yin broke. I never should have put them underneath her for safekeeping. It was the wrong place! I didn't get that job I wanted either, which is proof that my luck is doubly bad. I'm sorry, Lizzie, but I'm not going."

With that final word, Wai Gong picked up the two pieces of Guan Yin and took them to his bedroom. A few moments later, I heard a familiar song: "All I Want for Christmas Is You" by Mariah Carey. It wasn't even November yet.

CHAPTER NINE

"May the Force Be with Ewe"

Saturday had arrived! Comic Con was here in Glasgow. I was excited but also worried about our trip to Blackpool now that Wai Gong said he wasn't leaving the house again.

I'd done a little food shopping yesterday after school to make sure I was totally free to enjoy myself. Wai Gong was holed up in his room sulking, his music on loud. I'd texted Chi as soon as I woke up and told her Wai Gong didn't want to go to Blackpool anymore. She had messaged me back saying that he'd probably just had a bad day. We had a few weeks to persuade him to go to Blackpool. She was right. Tonight, he and I would watch *Strictly*, and he would realize how much we both needed this trip.

But right now, I had Comic Con to look forward to. I'd saved one pound a week for more than half a year so I could go. When I opened the door and saw Chi and Minh standing there—Princess Leia and Han Solo—I couldn't help but smile. They looked fantastic. I felt decidedly underdressed in my jeans and black sweatshirt. Minh looked fab as a young Solo in a brown leatherette jacket and black jeans. Chi looked brilliant with her hair in Princess Leia buns on the sides of her head.

"Wow, your hair is amazing," I said. I put out my hand to touch them, and she flinched.

"No, don't touch the hair buns, Lizzie!" She put her white hood carefully over her perfect hair. "I just want them to look perfect." I rolled my eyes.

"She spent three hours in the bathroom this morning. Some of us needed the toilet," Minh said.

"You can't rush perfection," Chi said.

"We need to get a move on. My mate Nathan is gonna meet me there. He's coming as Shang-Chi."

"Cool," I said.

"So, you're not dressing up today?" Minh said to me. "It's Comic Con, Lizzie, the first time it's ever been in Glasgow, and you aren't cosplaying? You could have gone as Xialing, Shang-Chi's sister, instead of wearing a sweatshirt that says . . . MAY THE FORCE BE WITH EWE? Is that a sheep?"

"Yes, it's a female sheep. Dressing up is not my thing," I said. "It's fine, I'm happy as I am." I looked down at the ground. Minh probably thought I was a total loser.

"If Lizzie doesn't want to cosplay, that's her decision. But you're happy you're coming, right?" Chi asked me.

73

I nodded. A day without having to look after Wai Gong or do the shopping was a big treat.

"Well, let's get going," Chi said. "We have to get the bus because his car, aka the Mini Orange, is getting tested, and I'm not sure it's going to pass."

"It's going to pass," said Minh, looking annoyed.

"Is there something wrong with your gramps?" Chi asked. She pointed up at our first-floor window. Wai Gong was staring at us with a strange look on his face. His eyes were wide as saucers.

"He's fine. Just seeing us off." I waved, and he pointed at us. I waved again.

He was mouthing something, but I couldn't make it out. Should I stay home? I felt guilty for going out and having fun, especially now that Wai Gong was determined not to leave the house.

Chi pulled my arm. "Come on, he'll be all right. Quick, run, the bus is coming!"

The bus pulled up to the stop and we got on. We tapped the card reader and went up to the top deck.

"Careful of my hair, you nearly hit a bun!" Chi snapped at Minh.

"Yes, Your Highness," said Minh.

I hoped they weren't going to bicker the whole day. We walked down the aisle to the back seats and sat down.

When we got to the exhibition center, Tyler was there. He slid on his Spock ears and greeted us with the Vulcan salute.

"Nope, Tyler, don't do your Vulcan mumbo jumbo at me!" Chi laughed. "Tell me where I can find the *Star Wars* stage, will you?"

"The crowd is huge by the *Star Wars* stage; you won't get to the front of it today," Tyler said. "I'm off to see a Klingon."

"Wait, let's meet up in a few hours and compare notes. We can see who got the most autographs! I bet I get more than Minh!" Chi said. Minh rolled his eyes.

"Sure, maybe around three we can meet up near the Studio Ghibli stage. I should be done with the Trekkies by then." Tyler ran off in the other direction.

"I'm going to leave you here," said Minh. "I will meet you at this cutout of Spider-Man at four o' clock. You've got my number, but don't tell Mum and Dad that I left you to wander about by yourselves, okay?"

Chi flicked her hand as if to say, *Be off with you, foul peasant!* and linked arms with me.

Being at Comic Con was surreal. There was a buzz of excitement in the air, and people had gone to such huge efforts to dress up. There was also a sense of freedom, that you could be whoever you wanted, be part of something bigger than yourself—a fandom, a universe, an alternative viewpoint. It felt good!

What I wasn't so great at was big crowds. Thousands of people bustled this way and that, and I was beginning to feel a bit hot. I held on to Chi's arm as she led me to look at the memorabilia stands. I didn't have money to buy anything, but at least I could look.

Just then, six Storm Troopers marched past, their white plastic armor reflecting the lights. Chi nudged me.

"Oh my god! They look so real!" she squealed with excitement. I grinned too. I felt my shoulders relax for the first time in ages.

"What should we go see first?" I asked excitedly. Chi got out the map and the list of panel discussions.

A group of *Star Wars* fans came and took a photo with her. I got out my phone to take photos of everything. It was a lovely way to spend a Saturday.

The whole place was buzzing with fans of comic book, TV, and film characters. It was the ultimate costume party. Some cosplayers had really spent a lot on their outfits; you could tell they'd had them professionally made. Others had used things they had at home. And I was happy to see that I wasn't the only person who hadn't dressed up. There were loads of people wearing regular clothes.

We spent hours wandering around taking photos and snapping selfies with cosplayers. When my feet began to ache a bit from the walking around, I was happy to sit on the floor and munch on the ham sandwich I'd brought with me. Chi lined up for an overpriced hot dog without ketchup, as she didn't want to risk getting any sauce on her costume.

It was time for us to head to the main stage for the panel talk we had been waiting for all day; one of the panelists was an actor from a *Star Wars* spinoff series, *The Mandalorian*, who Chi was particularly excited about seeing. She made me promise I would stand in line with her after so she could get his autograph in her book. We saw Minh over to the side with his friends Nathan and Ade from college. He gave us a little nod, but it was clear he didn't want us to go over there to hang out.

The panel was amazing. The actors made us laugh and talked about what it was like working on well-known film and TV franchises like Marvel and *Star Wars*. The actor who played Wong in *Doctor Strange* had a thick Northern accent. Seeing a row of East Asian actors up there made me feel proud. Chi shared my feelings—it meant so much to us to see East Asian superheroes and actors in the film and TV franchises we loved. It was one of the reasons Minh wanted to be a filmmaker and why Chi was thinking about becoming an actress. We all cheered and whooped when they finished talking.

"That was so awesome," gasped Chi as the crowd dispersed. We were on the hunt for autographs now.

"I can't believe we got to see them, Chi. I'm so glad I came!" I told her. I was having so much fun!

CHAPTER TEN

Meeting Our Heroes

Chi and I lined up to meet the actor who played Captain Carson Teva from *The Mandalorian*, but the queue was long. It was a bit boring, standing in line—we'd already been waiting at least twenty minutes, and my feet were starting to ache again. It was cool to meet actors and all, but I was not a mega-fan like Chi. For that, you had to have money or parents who had money to buy you all the merch. I just couldn't afford all that stuff.

I started to look around to see what else was going on. On the other side of the aisle behind the *Loki* area, I thought I saw someone who looked like Wai Gong; he had the same black hair and a red scarf. But it couldn't be. He wouldn't be at a place like this. I shook my head and turned back to Chi. We moved up toward the signing table, and now we only had a few people in front of us. But I had a nagging feeling.

"Chi, I've got to go check something out. I'll be right back," I told her.

I jogged over to the other side of the aisle, but now I couldn't see him. Was I hallucinating because I was tired? Just then, I felt a large hand grab me by the shoulder. I turned to see Wai Gong standing right behind me. He gave me a huge hug.

"Lizzie! I found you!" he said. He looked flustered, a bit like the other day when he couldn't find his keys. "Where is she?"

"Who? What? What are you doing here, Wai Gong?" I asked. "How did you get in? I thought you weren't going to leave the flat."

"I changed my mind, plus I found my wallet under my bed. I paid for a ticket over there by the big doors. They gave me an old person's discount—half price. And he called me 'pal.' I love being called that." He was distracted and peering over my shoulder. "You were with *her*."

"Who are you talking about?" I asked.

"The goddess, Guan Yin . . . I saw her with you."

I was really confused.

"Quick, there she is!" Wai Gong held my hand and ran over to where Chi was.

Chi nervously handed her autograph book to the actor. He smiled.

"Wow, you look great, Princess Leia!" he said.

"This is not a princess! This is the goddess, the goddess of compassion and mercy—Guan Yin!" Wai Gong declared from the side of the table.

"Sorry, dude, but I think you've got your icons mixed up," the actor said. I didn't know whether to laugh or cry at someone calling Wai Gong "dude."

"Goddess, I'm so happy you are here . . ." Wai Gong had his hands in a prayer position.

"Errr, Lizzie . . ." said Chi. Her face was starting to go red, and her makeup was becoming a little sweaty.

I patted Wai Gong on the arm as I turned to everyone who was staring at us.

"Don't mind him. That's just my grandfather. He likes to . . . erm . . . act a little," I said.

"That's why I wanted to work on the big screen!" said the actor. He finished signing Chi's *Mandalorian* memorabilia.

"I am happy that the goddess is here. She will help us overcome—we are no longer alone," Wai Gong said, nodding.

"That's good to know, dude," said the actor. "Nice to meet you all. Okay, see you." That was our cue to move out of the way.

I pulled Wai Gong over to a quiet corner. Chi followed a few steps behind, looking at her newly signed merch.

"Wai Gong, what are you doing here?" I whispered.

"I saw her outside the window of the flat. There she was in her flowing white robes—she's finally come to help us. Her hair is a little different, but it's definitely her." Wai Gong beamed. I hadn't seen him smile that wide in such a long time.

What? Wait a minute. Wai Gong thought Chi was real-life Guan Yin? I knew he hadn't seen Chi in a while, but still, this was bonkers, right? He peered around me and smiled at Chi.

"How can she be real, Wai Gong? Guan Yin is a statue, isn't she?"

"My grandmother told me once that the goddess visited her when my father died. She saw her, as real as I am seeing the goddess now."

I looked at Chi and back to Wai Gong. He really didn't recognize her as my best friend. I knew Tyler had done a good job with the Leia costume, and wearing the hood made Chi seem a little Guan Yin–like, but surely he could see it was my bestie?

"You don't think she looks like someone else you might know? Someone who likes *Star Wars*?"

Chi, not known for her patience, cleared her throat. I could see she was annoyed by the scowl on her face. I stood in front of Wai Gong, unsure if I was shielding him from the wrath of Chi or trying to stop him from embarrassing me.

"Lizzie, we can't spend the last bit of Comic Con with your grandad hanging around us. He's overdoing the acting stuff," Chi said. Wai Gong got down on his knees and bowed his head to the floor. "He's not doing it right either. Leia didn't have subjects who kowtowed like that."

I bent down and gently rubbed Wai Gong's back. I whispered in his ear, "Wai Gong, why don't you go home?" But he wasn't listening to me. "Please go home and listen to your CDs? We've got *Strictly* to look forward to this evening." Still no response; he remained like a boulder on the floor.

Chi mouthed, "What's going on?"

I shrugged. "I dunno, this is new," I told her.

"He's acting really strange," Chi said.

"I should take him home. Wai Gong, let's go," I said. But Chi grabbed my arm.

"No, you can't go yet. We said we'd meet up with the others and compare the autographs we got! I'm sure I have more than Minh, and we said we'd catch up with Tyler too. If he's come to take you home, he can wait a bit, right?" Chi let go of my arm and gently bent down next to Wai Gong. "Hey, Mr. Chu. Would you mind sitting down on that bench over there until Lizzie and I are finished? Then you can take her home."

He lifted himself up and nodded, then looked to where she was pointing.

"Sure thing, whatever you say," said Wai Gong, getting up and brushing off his jogging pants. "You're always full of wisdom!" He sauntered over to the bench and sat down. He was joined by a Spider-Man cosplayer who was adjusting his mask.

I couldn't believe it. "Wow, you got him to do that without protesting. What is happening?" I exclaimed. "I can't even get him to come to parents' evening."

She shrugged. "What can I say? I'm Princess Leia. I command a great army of rebels."

"I don't know if we should leave him here," I said. I imagined him trying to follow any Princess Leia who crossed his path. What if he got lost? He would be better off going home.

"Come on, Lizzie, relax! Have some fun. He'll be perfectly all right. You heard him. He'll just rest here for a bit."

"It's just—"

"Just nothing. You saved your money for ages to come here. You need to enjoy yourself. It's not your fault that he turned up."

No, it's yours, I wanted to say. *He followed you*. But I didn't say anything. He looked quite content next to the Spider-Man guy.

"Look, give him your phone. He can watch cute videos of cats or something."

I reluctantly took out my phone and connected to the convention center's Wi-Fi.

"Here, Wai Gong, you can watch some videos on my phone for a bit. We won't be too long. Just stay here, and we'll get you when we're finished." I found a YouTube video of cute cats doing silly things.

He took the phone and began to watch. He laughed and seemed happy enough to sit for a while and wait for me.

"Ha ha, this cat fears cucumbers. Ha ha ha! So funny!" he said.

Chi gave me a thumbs-up. "See, I told you. He's a grown adult. He will be fine, and then he can take you home when we're finished."

"Wai Gong, we'll come back soon. Stay here. Don't move," I told him. Chi linked her arm through mine.

"I am going to sit here," Wai Gong said, and he looked content. Thirty minutes wouldn't hurt, would it?

"He'll be fine," Chi said. "Come on!"

We ran off toward the Ghibli stage, where soot sprites were doing a dance.

Tyler was there alone. Despite Tyler and Chi not liking the same sci-fi franchises, we all loved Studio Ghibli films. My favorite was *My Neighbor Totoro*, and Chi and Tyler loved *Howl's Moving Castle*. The Ghibli stage was brilliant. You could take your photo with a huge inflatable Totoro on the side of the stage. The three of us all posed with peace-sign fingers.

"How many autographs did you get?" Tyler asked.

Chi looked through her bag at the stuff she'd gotten signed. "Maybe ten?"

"I wish I didn't have flat feet; they really hurt now," I told them. "Shall we go? I think it's starting to empty out."

"Yeah, I think we've seen everything we wanted to see," Chi said. "Let's go get your gramps and I can go meet up with Minh."

"Your gramps is here?" Tyler asked. "He didn't want you to be out by yourself?"

"No, it's not that. I think he wants to walk me home or something." I couldn't face having to explain the whole Wai Gong mistaking Chi for Guan Yin thing right now.

We went to where we had left him, but the bench no longer had a Spider-Man on it . . . or my grandad.

Wai Gong was gone.

"Where is he?" I did a 360-degree turn looking for him. "Let's go find him."

Chi, Tyler, and I ran around the convention hall looking for him. We found Minh and his friends, who also began helping us look for a Chinese man in his sixties wearing a red knitted scarf. The convention was winding down, and most people were milling toward the exits.

"I should have taken him straight home instead of leaving him there by himself," I said. "He was a bit confused."

"He must have gone home, Lizzie," Chi said. "I'll call your phone and see if he picks up." Chi got out her phone and called me. "He's not answering. Come on, we'll take you home, won't we, Minh?" Chi glared at her brother; it was more of a command than a question.

"Yeah, that was the plan anyway, wasn't it? Your grandad probably thought Comic Con wasn't for him," Minh said.

"Don't worry, Lizzie, he'll be fine. Minh's right. Let's go back to the West End. I'm sure he's there," said Tyler in his usual reassuring way, taking off his Vulcan ears.

"You're right. He probably just decided to go home," I said. "Come on, let's go."

CHAPTER ELEVEN

More Bad Luck

I rushed into the flat. My phone was on the table in the hall-way. I pulled my sneakers off and kicked them against the wall.

"Wai Gong! Where are you?" I yelled. I ran into the living room. He was sitting on the sofa with his feet resting on a stool. He was eating a cookie.

"Why didn't you wait on the bench? I told you we'd be back to get you," I said. "We were looking all over the place for you."

"I'm sorry, Lizzie, but that bench was terribly hard. It was made of wood, and the Spider fella, he told me there were more comfortable seats in another area, so I followed him. But then I thought I spotted the goddess, but it wasn't her. She had the same white robe, but she was holding a gun, and Guan Yin never holds weapons. Then I spotted this group of people dressed like strange creatures, so I had to get out of there. I found a different bench, and I was waiting for you there because I couldn't remember how to get back to the other place. I was hoping the goddess would come back and guide me, but she didn't return. So I left."

"Wai Gong, you worried me silly! I didn't have my phone with me. You can't do this kind of thing when we go to Blackpool, you know. You can't just wander off and not tell me where you're going. It's different from Glasgow. I know you know your way around here, but there you need to stay close to me." I thought if I just made it seem like we were going, he might change his mind.

"Ah, I see what you are doing, Lizzie. But I already told you, I am not going to Blackpool. I wanted to, but breaking the goddess statue is bad luck. Look at today—I was coming to meet you and the goddess, but then you disappeared. Putting the tickets underneath my beloved goddess was my mistake, and I will suffer the consequences. Today was another sign: I need to stay at home. Don't you see?"

"I don't get it, Wai Gong, I really don't. The trip is a gift from Grandma Kam, and that's what you should be focusing on. Not the silly goddess."

"Come, Lizzie, let's have a good evening together. We've got *Strictly* tonight!"

He was sort of right. I had to get dinner prepared, and then I would try again to discuss the Blackpool idea. He had to come. There was no way I was letting him not go! He needed this, even if he didn't know it yet.

I cooked instant noodles and added some chicken I had fried and bok choy I had bought yesterday. I slurped the soup from the side of the bowl and then shoveled the chicken and noodles into my mouth. Wai Gong got the remote and put on *Strictly Come Dancing*. I wasn't going to let him say no a third time. But what could I do to change his mind?

The dancers came on-screen. It was movie week. The professional dancers were dressed in angel and devil costumes. Milo du Peck was a human who was being pulled from side to side by his conscience, which was personified by the devils and angels. One of the devils was trying to get him to do what he wanted, but an angel wouldn't let him and said something sweet that made him smile. Wai Gong clapped his hands.

I knew what some of the moves were called now that I had been watching ballroom and Latin dance videos on my phone. Brian from New York was a terrific online coach. This girl from Glasgow was starting to enjoy learning new steps.

"Wow, did you see that paso doble part they put in there?" I asked.

"I hope they put a reverse fleckerl in tonight's Viennese waltz. I know Milo du Peck loves a good fleckerl," Wai Gong said. He still loved *Strictly* and dancing. How could I possibly change his mind about going to Blackpool? It was clear to me that dancing made him happy. Why would he stop himself from being happy? I just didn't get it.

Suddenly, one of the dancers dressed as an angel opened her wings wide. A path made of bright lights lit up down the middle of the dance floor, and the guardian angel walked slowly down it. The main devil was on his knees, gradually looking less devilish: He removed his horns, and under his black cape he gave his outfit one strong tug. All of it came off, and underneath he was wearing a stunning white tuxedo. He started to tap-dance with glee.

"Wah! It's so good, Lizzie—look how she's taking him down the good path!" Wai Gong said, on the edge of his seat. "It's good to have guidance from the divine. It's why I trust Guan Yin, you see; she guides me in the right direction!"

I looked at Wai Gong and then back to the screen. *Divine guidance, eh?*

Suddenly, I knew exactly how I was going to get Wai Gong to Blackpool!

CHAPTER TWELVE

One Goddess, Coming Up!

I was pacing up and down the living room to keep warm and because I was nervous. I'd put on three pairs of socks and my flip-flops because it was so cold. I also put on the necklace Grandma Kam had given me. Jade was lucky, apparently. Would this bonkers idea work?

I'd texted Chi to come over. She was due any moment. I looked out of the window to the street and saw Chi's head and her red raincoat.

The buzzer went off, and I ran to the intercom and pushed the button to let her in. I went to the front door.

"Hey, thanks for asking me to come over. You've done me a big favor. Mum was starting to talk about me helping in the café at lunchtime, washing up, but I told her you had an emergency. Minh is going to work instead. He's annoyed with me, but that's not new. What's up?"

"Thanks so much for coming. Did you bring your Leia costume?"

"I did, but it needs washing. I'm not naming names, but someone got some sweet chili on the bottom of it. Okay, I am naming names. It was Minh. The oaf was holding the bottle above my head and wouldn't give it to me, so I grabbed it and some of it fell onto my Leia outfit. You're so lucky, Lizzie, that you don't have an annoying big brother to deal with!"

I didn't tell Chi that I wished I had more family around me like she did. Even though she and Minh argued a lot, I knew they really loved each other. She wanted to be like him, hence her *Star Wars* fandom. It was a way she could get closer to her brother even though there was an age gap of six years.

"I'm sure the sauce will come out in the wash." I'd done enough laundry to know that you could get most stains out if you tried. "Come with me to my grandad's room," I said.

We walked down the hallway to Wai Gong's room. He was out.

"What's this all about, then?" Chi asked. I motioned for her to sit on the bed.

"It's to do with *her*." I pointed to the statue pieces on the bedside table. Wai Gong still hadn't managed to put them back together. His supergluing had been super unsuccessful.

"You want me to try and fix that?" she said, still looking confused as to why she was here.

"Nope, I need a *big* favor," I said. In true Lizzie style, it made me uncomfortable asking Chi for help. Wai Gong and Grandma Kam had been firm: We did things by ourselves, and we didn't impose on others or "lose face." Chi had already let me have an impromptu birthday party at her place.

"Are you about to tell me something I don't want to hear?" she said. "What's up? Spit it out."

"Well . . . I've not been able to sleep because I'm worried about what happened yesterday at Comic Con. I've got a massive favor to ask you, but I want to tell you a story first. One about this goddess my grandad worships."

"All right . . . you really are scaring me a little. You look so serious," Chi said.

"This is a story Wai Gong told me, and I want to tell it to you because I need you to do something for me."

I took a deep breath. I hoped I remembered the story correctly.

Guan Yin Saves the Village

A long time ago, a gang of terrible men overran a small seaside village where fishing was the main trade. The local people were upset and scared; the men were stealing their food and creating chaos and fear wherever they went. The villagers didn't know what to do.

The goddess Guan Yin was determined to help. She knew she would have to make herself look like someone else, a person the leader of the gang would warm to. She knew that he might not listen to a goddess, but he would listen to a simple fisherwoman, as his mother had been. She transformed herself into a strong and beautiful fisherwoman who carried a wicker basket and wore a magnetic smile.

The leader of the gang instantly took to her. In fact, he wanted to marry her. But Guan Yin, in the guise of the fisherwoman, declined his advances. She told him that he would have to change his ways and learn the Buddhist scripture, give up meat, and discard his weapons, and only then would everyone be truly happy. The leader did as the fisherwoman asked. He convinced his gang to change their ways as well. They too were tired of living lives full of danger and sadness. They laid down their arms and stopped eating meat.

The village was a peaceful place to live once more. The gang become good citizens, and Guan Yin become the patron saint of fishermen and sailors. That's why she is often seen with a basket made of willow. She showed them that transformation was possible and that even seemingly bad people can change if someone who cares for them helps guide them to a new path.

Chi looked at me with eyebrows raised. "I don't get it. Why did she need to change into a different kind of woman? And I'm already a reluctant vegan. What is it you want, Lizzie?" Chi asked me.

"She changed her appearance to help others. She knew that the man would only listen to a certain kind of woman, one he trusted. It's my long-winded way of asking if you would do me the biggest favor by . . . by becoming a Chinese goddess for a day. *That* Chinese goddess, to be specific." I pointed to the broken Guan Yin statue.

"Become a goddess for a day? What are you talking about? Is that what your gramps was going on about yesterday?" Chi said.

I nodded. "You know Wai Gong has been acting a little odd lately. He wasn't at Comic Con to take me home. He was there because he saw you dressed as Princess Leia with your white hood and thought you were Guan Yin come to life! I know it sounds ridiculous, but it's true. He said his grandma saw her too back in China, that one night the goddess visited her."

"So let me get this straight: He thought I was *that* goddess statue over there, the one that's broken. And that's why he was acting like I was all powerful and mighty?"

"Yes." I gulped, unsure of how to proceed. I knew it sounded unbelievable. "He's told me twice that he isn't going to go to Blackpool. That he thinks breaking the statue brought bad luck. I think the only way to get him there is if Guan Yin goes too. In the story, the goddess changed into a fisherwoman. I'm asking you, dear bestie, to go from schoolgirl to goddess. She's the only person he will listen to. He's so sad about Grandma Kam that he's not thinking straight."

"Yeah, that makes sense," Chi said, picking up the top part of the broken goddess statue. She turned it around in her hands and used her index finger to follow the long black strands of hair cascading down the front of Guan Yin's chest.

"I know that taking him to the Blackpool Tower is going to make him better," I carried on. "I'm learning the cha-cha so I can re-create the good times he had with my grandma." I felt a lump form in my throat. "I've got a feeling that things are changing, and I'll regret it forever if I don't do this. Tyler was right—it was her final wish."

I searched Chi's face for a hint at what she might say. Her lips puckered; her brow furrowed. She was thinking hard. Just then, the front door buzzer rang.

"That'll be Tyler," Chi said.

"I'll go let him in," I told her as I ran out of the room.

I let Tyler in, and he followed me to my grandfather's room. I sat on the bed next to Chi.

"Hey, you two, why the serious faces?" Tyler asked.

"I've just asked Chi if she'll be a goddess for a day," I said.

"Okay, that sounds like something Chi would be into," Tyler said. "I'm all ears. Tell me more!"

"I don't know if I am into it, though. I love dressing up, but this is a whole new level!" Chi said. "I can't decide. Ty, help me figure it out! You're always our voice of reason!"

"What does that mean though, to be a goddess for a day? Is it a weird *Star Wars* thing?" Tyler asked.

"It's not a weird *Star Wars* thing! We'll be helping someone. My grandad thinks that Chi here is his favorite goddess, Guan Yin, when she dresses up in the Princess Leia costume. He said someone in his family was visited by the goddess in the past. And he talks to her all the time—well, he did, but he broke his statue of her, and now he thinks Chi is the living incarnation of his goddess," I said with hardly a breath in between words.

"Complicated!" Tyler said. "If we're helping someone, I don't see why there would be a problem. You've been through a lot in the past year, and maybe this is what you all need. My dad says kindness is a superpower. Chi, do you think we can help spread a little kindness Lizzie's way?"

Chi nodded. "Of course! Plus, I've always wanted to get into acting; this could be my first major role."

I laughed. Typical Chi!

"I could get my nails done. But I want ribbons like she's got on her robe. And I want my hair up in that cool style with the gold thing at the front." Chi picked up the two pieces of the statue and put the goddess together.

"You'll do it?" I said. I couldn't believe it.

"Yes! You know how much I love to dress up, *and* we'll get to go to Pleasure Beach too. We can get one of those photos they take of people on roller coasters, and we can have our hands up! And I will look amazing! I'm so excited!" Chi gently put Guan Yin back on the bedside table.

"Thanks so much, Chi, you're a total star," I said. I grabbed Chi and gave her the biggest hug. "Tyler, would you help us update the costume?"

"Definitely!" Tyler spread out the Leia costume on the bed, then looked at the statue. "A little mauve ribbon here. A little tuck there. Easy." He laughed.

"So let's get this right. I'm going to be playing Gwen Yin," Chi said.

"Guan Yin," I corrected her. "In Cantonese, it's Gwun Yam."

"Gu-an Yin. Cool," Chi said. She scrolled on her phone. "But here it's spelled Kuan Yin . . . and on this page, Kwan Yin."

"Yeah, it's the same goddess but different spellings," I told her.

"She's the goddess of being kind and stuff like that?" Chi asked, squinting. "You know what, I think my dad knows about her."

"I wouldn't be surprised. He's Vietnamese; they have the same gods."

"Has she got magical powers?" Tyler asked. "Like She-Ra?"

"No! Well . . . kinda. She's the goddess of compassion and mercy. You said being nice is a superpower, right? And that's why Chi will be the bestest kind goddess," I said. I looked at Tyler and raised my eyebrows.

Tyler began to laugh. He held his hand up to his mouth.

"What's so funny?" Chi demanded, looking annoyed.

"Chi, c'mon, you have to admit that's funny. You're not really the most *compassionate* person in the whole wide world, are you?" Tyler said.

"Hey!" Chi objected. "I'm definitely that word. Compassionate!" She turned to me. "It means I'm caring, right?"

"Yes," I told them. "Chi can be caring. She just needs to like you first." We all laughed.

"That's true, I suppose," said Chi. "But I don't need to like lots of people when I have the two finest human specimens in the entire universe right here."

"We still haven't figured out how we're actually going to get to Blackpool, have we?" Tyler asked. "Flying carpet? Skateboard? National Express?"

"I know! What if Minh takes us?" Chi said. "He's got a car. And it would be an easier sell if my mum knew he was going with us. That way we could go door to door in a car too, so we can keep an eye on Wai Gong and he can't wander off."

"Do you think he would take us though?" I asked. "He seems quite busy working at the café and with his film stuff."

"Minh's at work right now. You go and ask him. He likes you. And if it's a no, then I can try to convince him."

"That sounds like a plan," I said.

"Are you ready, Ty?" Chi asked.

"Let me take a photo first. Chi, hold the goddess pieces together so I have a reference to work from," Tyler said.

Chi did as he asked and held the head and shoulders onto the rest of the goddess's body. She looked very serene despite being in two pieces. Tyler took out his phone and snapped a photo. Then they both got up and left with plans to turn the Leia costume into a celestial outfit fit for a goddess.

I got out my phone and typed into the notes section:

Things to do before our journey to Blackpool:

Ask Chi to be a goddess for the day to help convince Wai Gong to go—CHECK

Do at least two more YouTube dance lessons—ONGOING

Ask Minh if he will drive us in the Mini Orange—TO DO

Raise money for gas and food—TO DO

Convince Wai Gong that Guan Yin wants him to go to Blackpool—TO DO

I touched Grandma Kam's jade necklace. It had made me lucky so far today. I hoped it would carry on when I asked Minh if he would be our driver.

CHAPTER THIRTEEN

Soya Bean Café

After I finished another YouTube cha-cha session in my bedroom (I was getting the hang of the first bit now), I walked over to Soya Bean Café. Byres Road was heaving with students and shoppers, but the lane was particularly quiet. I opened the door to the café and walked in. Minh was leaning on the counter talking to the cook, Kai, through a rectangular hole in the wall. There was only one couple slurping noodle soup in the corner. Minh heard the bell and turned around.

"Hey, Lizzie, what are you doing here? Chi's not here. She's at home, probably painting her nails," Minh said.

"It's you I wanted to talk to, actually," I said. I felt awkward asking my friend's brother for a massive favor. "Can we sit down?"

Minh nodded. The barstools by the counter weren't the easiest to climb up on, but I managed to get up and swiveled around to face Minh. He was looking at me with an odd expression on his face.

"Lizzie, I'm loads older than you, so if you're hoping to go on a date . . ." Minh said, his cheeks going red.

"Ewwww! No way! Minh! I'm not here to ask you out!" I wanted to crawl into a hole and hide. "As *if*! I'm only twelve!"

"Oh, sorry, Lizzie, I just thought . . ." Minh looked sheepish. A laugh came from the kitchen.

"Very cool, bro!" Kai said.

"What do you want, Lizzie?"

I took a deep breath.

"Minh, I've got a big favor to ask you. I need you to drive my grandad, Chi, Tyler, and me to Blackpool in two weeks' time. My grandma left me tickets for afternoon tea at the Blackpool Tower Ballroom, and we need a lift. Please, would you take us?"

"Erm . . ." He frowned. "It just doesn't sound like my cup of tea—old biddies dancing around, eating fancy cut sandwiches. You can get a bus or a train from here. Your grandad should be able to watch you three, shouldn't he?"

It felt like my stomach had been hit by a bull. I didn't want to tell him the real reason why this was important for Wai Gong and me.

"I can make it worth your while," I said. "I can get tickets to Pleasure Beach—it's got amazing roller coasters. I'll pay for fish and chips on the seafront, and you'd get extra brownie points with your mum and dad for being a good big brother." I was desperate for anything that would convince Minh to be our driver.

"All of that actually sounds quite good, but spending three hours in my car with Chi jabbering on . . . I don't think I can hack that part of it, if I'm being honest."

"Oh, please, Minh. You know how you and Chi loved Comic Con because you're big *Star Wars* fans? Well, it's the same for fans of Latin dance and ballroom. My grandad loves dancing so much, and we really want to take him there. He really needs this to get over my grandma passing away."

"I'm sorry, Lizzie, it's still a no," Minh said.

The door opened and a little bell tinkled. Chi came in. She looked at me with her eyebrows raised, and I shook my head to tell her he'd said no.

"Sorry I'm late, Lizzie . . . hey, fabulous older brother of mine," Chi said, sidling up to the counter and climbing onto the seat next to mine. I was doubtful that Chi's puppy-dog-eyes routine would work on Minh. She was known for being super persuasive with other people, but not with her own brother. I crossed my fingers on my lap and scrunched my toes in anticipation.

"Have you come to gloat because you don't have to work here like I do?" Minh said, wiping down the counter with a wet cloth.

Chi looked at me and then swiveled to face her brother.

"Minh, I can tell from Lizzie's face that you've said no to Blackpool. What if we buy you loads of Blackpool rock candy and cotton candy?" Chi asked.

Minh shook his head. "Nope, doesn't sound worth it." He was driving a hard bargain. I couldn't think what else we could offer to make him come with us.

"Come on, Chi, we tried," I said, tugging on her arm. "Let's just go. I'll find another way to get us there." I stood up.

Chi looked at her brother with an intense stare. She was calculating something in that head of hers.

"You need to film a documentary to get into that film school, right?"

"What if I do?" Minh said. He was paying attention now. He crossed his arms, but his head was tilted to the side as if he wanted to hear more. I sat back down.

"What if you filmed the trip to Blackpool? We could help by filming on our phones too. What about this tag line for a short film? 'Lonely old widower given the trip of a lifetime for one last waltz'?" Chi was holding her hands out like you see in the movies when people are trying to sell something. She was emitting used car salesperson vibes. I didn't want to interrupt to tell her that I was learning the cha-cha, not the waltz.

Minh looked at his kid sister. This was promising; he hadn't immediately cut her off or told her to go home.

"Maybe . . ." he said. "I could film sad vignettes on the beach. Close-ups of Mr. Chu pining for his dead wife . . . Oh, that's very filmic—the rolling waves of the sea, the decay of an English seaside town, the tears of a lonely man. The granddaughter wishing her grandmother hadn't died. The old man longing for a love lost, the dance that will save the day . . ." I felt a little uncomfortable when Minh put it like that. "Sorry, Lizzie, I got carried away."

"We're all going to be dressed up in flashy clothes too," Chi said. She didn't mention the goddess. There was no way Minh would take us if he knew about Wai Gong thinking Chi was a goddess come to life. "Come on, Minh, I know you've been looking for something to film for ages. This could get you that placement you want, which means you can leave home and go follow your filmmaker dreams. And the big bonus is that you get a day off from working here." Minh's face lit up.

"Actually, that would all be great footage for a documentary short. I hate to say this, Chi, but I think you are on to something. I suppose I could do it . . . but how many tickets have you got for the Tower?" he asked me.

"Four," I told him.

"There'd be five of us," he calculated, using his fingers.

"We could sneak you into the Tower and you could film from the balcony," Chi said quickly, not even knowing if that was possible. I looked at her. She shrugged, and her eyes told me I should just go with the flow. I simply nodded.

Minh held out his hand for me to shake. I took it and shook it. Chi grinned and held her hand out toward her brother, but Minh left her hanging. She stuck her tongue out.

"Count me in, Lizzie—I'll need gas money and food," he said. A group of students came in and sat down at a table near the window. "Now get out of here. I have to work."

Chi and I hopped down from our stools and linked arms as we left Soya Bean Café.

"You did it, Chi!" I said, giving her arm a squeeze. I took out my phone and put a check next to the third item on my list.

We had a driver and wheels!

CHAPTER FOURTEEN

The Phams

We had a couple of weeks to raise the money we needed. Wai Gong had taken some of the cash I'd saved for emergencies to get into Comic Con, and we needed money for gas, food, and Pleasure Beach tickets before we even left Glasgow. I had made a budget, and if we all ate homemade sandwiches on the way there and took water bottles, we'd need around two hundred pounds. But Chi said we should raise more so we could eat out. We decided two hundred and fifty pounds would be enough.

I was at the Phams' doing my homework with Chi when Minh came home, and we decided to tell their parents about our plans. Tay and Jane were sitting at the kitchen table drinking green tea from a see-through teapot.

"Mum, I've got something I want to ask you," Chi said. She looked at me for support. I gave her a little smile. "For Lizzie's birthday, she got tickets to afternoon tea at the Blackpool Tower Ballroom. It's her grandad's favorite place. And luckily, Tyler and I are invited too."

"Yes?" Jane said. I could tell from her face that she was a little suspicious now.

"Minh has agreed to take us in his car. And Mr. Chu will be there too, so we'll have two adults with us."

"You agreed to this?" Jane asked Minh, surprised. "I thought you hated babysitting Chi on outings."

"Not all the time," said Minh.

"When is it?" Tay asked.

"Not this Sunday, but the one after," I said.

"In two weeks? I need Minh to work that weekend," Jane told us.

"Come on, Mum, let me take them. It's for Lizzie and her grandad," Minh said.

"It's just for one day, Mum," said Chi. "And you're always saying that Minh needs to keep an eye on me more. I've got to go because Lizzie's gran left Tyler and me tickets. Please, can Minh take us in his car?"

"I don't know if it can do a trip like that on the highway. It's an old car, Minh," Tay said.

"It just passed its test," said Minh. "I'm sure it'll be fine."

"At your pal's garage," Tay said. "You should take it to that place near the community garden instead. They're very good with older classic cars. It needs a pair of expert eyes, not just any old mechanic."

"Stop worrying, Dad. It passed, and that's all that matters."

"Yeah, Dad, his car is going to be fine," Chi added.

"It's unusual for you to stand up for him," Tay said to her. "Well, if this is how you're going to act while you're out, I say you should go and have a bit of fun together."

Jane looked at everyone. "Oh, all right then. I'll cover Minh's shift that day, or I can ask Kai's sister—she was looking for some work. Do you want me to pack you some food?" Jane asked.

"No thanks!" Chi and Minh shouted in unison. I laughed as I remembered the brown birthday sludge.

"We can get food on the way there. We don't want to make more work for you, Mum," said Minh.

"We *do* need money though, 'cause we want to go to Pleasure Beach and go on some rides before we get to the Tower," Chi said. "Would you two like to donate to the Blackpool Fund?" Chi put her hands under her chin and did her pleading face. Her parents had just shelled out for her and Minh's Comic Con tickets.

"That sounds less about Lizzie's grandad and more about you wanting to go on roller coasters and bumper cars," said Tay. "I'm not sure we can spare any extra money this month. What do you think, Jane?" Tay looked at his wife and lifted his eyebrows.

"Tay's right. I'm sorry, Lizzie. Things are a little bit tight right now. You can go if you can raise the money yourselves though," she suggested. "It will be good for you to be more enterprising, Chi. It's good for girls to see women being entrepreneurs, like me."

Chi scrunched up her face.

"Sorry about my parents, Lizzie. They have their own ways of doing things," Minh said.

"If you had tastier food on your café menu, you'd get more customers," Chi said. Jane grimaced.

I needed to defuse the tension before there was another Pham family argument.

"We could do a car wash or bake sale?" I said, looking at Chi. I felt bad that I was messing up Jane's work schedule by asking Minh to take us on a road trip.

"Okay, I've got an idea," Chi said to her mum. "What if you lend us the parking spaces at the back of the café? We could usher cars down the lane to be washed. You've got an outdoor tap there, haven't you?" She was full of good ideas today.

"That's not a bad idea, Chi," said Minh. "I can post it on my socials to let people know."

"Yes, we'd be so grateful," I said. "I don't want the trip to be just about my grandad and me. I want these two and Tyler to have a good time as well, and that's why we're going to have a few hours at Pleasure Beach." I looked hopefully at Jane and Tay.

Tay took a swig of his tea and poured more into Jane's cup. They looked at each other and raised their eyebrows in silent communication across the table.

"Okay, Lizzie," Jane said. "You can use the parking spaces and the tap outside too. Just let me know when."

"How about tomorrow?" I asked. Chi and Minh both looked at me with wide eyes.

"Sure," said Jane.

"See? The universe always provides a way," said Tay, spouting his usual positive vibes. "Is your grandad feeling better now? I'm glad you got this trip to Blackpool for your birthday and he didn't forget after all. I hardly see him these days."

I didn't correct him and say that Grandma Kam had planned this trip for us or that Wai Gong wasn't his usual self lately. Would they let Minh and Chi go if I told them everything? I wasn't so sure.

"Yes, he's got his little hobbies. He likes to collect CDs and be out and about." I left out the talking to Chinese deities and showing up at Comic Con and my hope that going to Blackpool would cure him of his sadness, missing parents' evenings, and misplacing his keys.

Tay took out a bill from his back pocket. "Here you go, Lizzie—here's a tenner for your fundraiser." Jane raised her eyebrows. "What? It's just to start them off."

"Thanks, Tay!" I said, taking the ten pounds and putting it in my pocket. I felt good that I'd raised some money already!

Foamy Fun

The next day, we met up outside Soya Bean Café. We'd made some cardboard signs.

HEY! DIRTY CARS—GET IN HERE NOW!
YOUR CAR IS DIRTY AND YOU KNOW IT!
WASH IT!
DIRTY CAR, DIRTY SOUL
WASH THAT THING!

Tyler had asked his *Star Trek* friends from school to come and help for an hour or two. We'd bought buckets from home, and Chi had convinced a local supermarket to donate a bag of cleaning cloths, car soap, and sponges.

"You can use the outside tap as long as you aren't in the way of customers getting takeout," said Jane. "I'm not expecting any food deliveries, so this area is all yours. Make sure you turn off the tap when you're not using the water though. We don't want to be wasteful."

"Mum, it's fine, we're not totally useless," said Chi. She was wearing gold steampunk goggles and pink rubber gloves that were too big. Every time she pulled one up, the other one would fall on the floor.

"Why have you got those on?" Tyler asked. He was wearing a sensible tracksuit.

"I've just had my nails done. A French manicure. I figured a goddess would have perfect nails, and I don't want to ruin them. And I don't want to get soap in my eyes."

I'd made a fund-o-meter out of cardboard like the ones on TV. I colored in the line at the ten-pound mark. Only 240 pounds to go.

Tyler stood on the corner and held up a big cardboard sign, as he didn't want to get his hands soapy. He was good at rounding up customers.

OLD PEOPLE NEED FUN TOO!
only £5 for a car wash

His dad George had posted about it in the local neighborhood group on Facebook, and Minh had put posts up on his socials too.

Minh turned up in his Mini and honked his horn to get past the car washers. Soapsuds flew, and some landed on his windshield. He turned off his engine and got out.

"Hey, Lizzie. Hey, sprout—don't go scaring our customers away! Can you wash the Mini Orange too, please?"

"Don't call me sprout!" Chi said, jabbing her brother on the forearm. "And no! Do it yourself!" She threw a sponge at him.

"Owww! Oh, that's going to cost you, sprout! You must do everything I say on the trip because I'm the one driving."

"As if!" Chi said. "You're not in charge of me. You're merely the taxi driver!"

"Taxi driver!" Minh said. "You wouldn't be able to go if I weren't going too. Do you want me to tell Mum I've changed my mind and I can work next Sunday?"

Chi scowled at her brother. "Don't you dare," she said, pinching his arm with her rubber-covered fingers.

"Oww! I'm going to get you for that, sprout!" Minh said as he chased her around a post.

"Hello? Can you two please stop bickering for just one second? We need to start washing cars," Tyler said, rolling his eyes.

In the end, we washed forty-two cars and two delivery vans. One guy said we were a third cheaper than the place he normally went to and we probably could have asked for ten pounds a car instead. I didn't tell Tyler and Chi that we could have charged double and washed half the number of cars!

We had our goddess, we had our ride, and now the money was rolling in. Next, we needed to persuade Wai Gong that we were all going to Blackpool, and I knew just the goddess to do it. I just hoped it was going to work!

CHAPTER SIXTEEN

Fake Goddess to the Rescue

Tyler and Chi were on their way over for the goddess's first outing. Wai Gong was resting in his room with the door closed, soul music playing, so it seemed like a good time to see if my plan was going to work. My hands were sweating as I laid out on my bed the accessories I'd found for Chi. Tyler had sent me a photo of the robe—he'd been working on it at home. He'd locked it away in George's sewing room so it wouldn't get eaten by a playful Bishop. He'd done a pretty good job even though he didn't have a pattern to work from. We had loads of visual references to go by. He'd reused some of the Princess Leia costume and found some old net curtains at his auntie's place. They were a bit dusty, but after a wash, they scrubbed up nicely. There was also some leftover satin from Chi's parents' old duvet, and Tyler had sewn some mauve and gold ribbon around the edges.

I'd rummaged through Grandma Kam's trinket boxes and found a golden flower brooch. The statue of Guan Yin wore something like that in her hair, and she had a veil, long like a white waterfall. She was barefoot too. I didn't think I'd be able to convince Chi to walk around barefoot, as she had a complex about a wart on the top of her pinkie toe, so I had spray-painted an old pair of slippers metallic silver and added some sequins. That's what I imagined goddesses would wear on their feet. I put everything on my bed and held my breath as the door opened.

"Fake goddess coming atcha!" Chi said as she came inside. Tyler followed with a garment bag.

Chi's eyes immediately went from me to the things laid out on the bed. Tyler hung up the garment bag and unzipped it. He carefully got out Chi's recycled outfit. The ribbons and lace netting really made it heavenly.

Chi picked up the hairpieces and held them up. "How many hairpieces do you have here? A hundred?" She laughed, eyeing the long black synthetic hair I'd bought from the market. "I'm going to look so lush!"

"It's actually three wigs—well, a main wig and two hairpieces." I went over to her and sat her down on my bed.

Tyler laughed and began to put them on his head. He looked like Cousin Itt from *The Addams Family*, as his whole face was covered. Chi began to laugh.

"I'm trying to look serene and peaceful like Chi." Tyler laughed. He held up his phone, displaying a picture of the demure and kind goddess.

"Cheeky!" shouted Chi, punching Tyler in the arm.

"I've got this gold brooch for your hair—that goes here," I said, tapping the middle of her crown. "The veil attaches to the back."

"Okay . . . but Lizzie, what happens if your gramps recognizes me? What do I say to him then?" Chi said. "I'm not going to get into trouble for tricking an old man, am I?"

"Just be nice, Chi, and tell him you wanted to help him. That's the whole point of Lizzie's mission, isn't it? To help him feel better?" Tyler said. "My dads both tell me to treat people as I would want to be treated."

"Exactly," I said, "and I don't think he will know it's you. He didn't recognize you even when we didn't have the full costume. He said his grandma was visited by Guan Yin in China, so he really believes it's possible."

"I've heard stories of people who believe in miracles and, like, see Jesus's face in things," Tyler said.

"Maybe it's just a phase," Chi said.

"Maybe after our trip, he can just be normal again," I said.

"I hope so, Lizzie," said Tyler. "I'm looking forward to it regardless."

Chi picked up Tyler's phone, which still had the picture of Guan Yin on the screen. "I do kinda look like her, don't I? Her makeup is cool." She scanned the image more closely. "But I don't have a twig or one of those bottles. What are they for, Lizzie?"

"The willow branch signifies flexible but unbreakable strength, and the bottle means good fortune. I've already got those. Look, I've got this privet twig for the willow branch and an empty bottle of Perrier. I've peeled the sticker off," I told her.

"You've thought of everything, haven't you?" Chi said. I nodded.

We got Chi ready for her first performance as the goddess Guan Yin. She put on the robe and the long black hairpieces. Then I put the golden brooch into her hair at the front and pinned the white veil to the back of it. Chi stared at herself as she transformed. She sat a little taller, and her eyes softened. She stroked the veil as it cascaded down the side of her face. Tyler was a steady hand with the eyeliner and lip pencil. The face powder made her skin seem much brighter, and it sparkled slightly in the light.

"I feel more peaceful just wearing this costume," Chi said quietly. "Is that strange?"

"I don't think so at all," Tyler said. "I mean, clothes and costumes always make us feel certain ways. It's why you liked dressing up as Princess Leia. You channeled that character—that's what cosplay is, right?"

"Stand up," I said. Chi got up carefully and did a twirl. The brooch was heavy and flopped down, and the hairpieces swung around and whipped her in the eye. The veil slumped to the left of Chi's face in a lopsided protest.

"Whoa! Careful. You're going to have to be demure, I'm afraid—small movements, or the veil and hairpieces might move. Keep your head upright and move very, very slowly . . ." I readjusted the hair and accessories on her head.

"I feel strange," said Chi. She began to swirl her arms around, the satin of her robe shimmering in the light. "I guess I feel more goddess-like if I wave my arms around like this."

Tyler stifled a laugh.

"Well, all I can say is that you look like an angry goddess rather than a compassionate one. Smile a bit!" Tyler joked.

Chi bared her teeth a little too much; she looked like the Joker.

"Tone it down!" Tyler suggested. "You don't want to scare the poor guy. You're a goddess, not a vampire!"

"Look, you said smile, and I smiled," Chi said.

"It's fine, forget the smile," laughed Tyler.

I helped Chi make her way to Wai Gong's bedroom. The song "We Are Family" blared from behind his door. This was it.

CHAPTER SEVENTEEN

Is He Dead?

I knocked on Wai Gong's bedroom door. Nothing. I knocked again, then I decided to open the door anyway. I turned the handle, and the three of us peeked in. The music was loud. Wai Gong was lying flat on his bed, not moving. Chi looked at me, worried.

"Do you think he's . . . you know . . . dead?" she asked.

I gulped. He couldn't be dead, could he? I gently prodded his upper arm. Chi and Tyler stood next to me, leaning over a very still Wai Gong.

"Check if he's breathing," Tyler said. "Put your finger under his nose and see if you can feel him exhale."

I began moving my finger toward Wai Gong's face to do as Tyler had suggested. Chi rushed forward and put her mani- cured hand on his belly.

"He's not dead!" Chi shouted just as "We Are Family" finished. "His stomach's going up and down! He's breathing."

Just then, Wai Gong sat straight up, his eyes wide open. He looked at Chi in her goddess form. He smiled that same smile I'd seen when we were at Comic Con, the smile that had been missing for such a long time.

"Am I dreaming? It's a miracle, she's really here in our home!" Wai Gong said. "My grandma was right; she comes to you when you need her the most!" He jumped out of bed and knelt before Chi, whose mouth was agape. "I was listening to the music, and then all of a sudden, you are here. Guan Yin, I knew you wouldn't let me down."

Chi held out her hand like a queen.

"My esteemed, devoted . . . er . . . worshipper guy?" she said. I grimaced. She was being a bit of a weird goddess. She needed poise and a kind nature, and instead she was just being Chi but with a posh voice! She turned to me and said behind her hand, "I'm not very good at this, am I?"

I shook my head.

"See if you can channel Princess Leia with a side of Michelle Obama. Be kind, but have a commanding presence . . . something like that?" Tyler whispered to her.

"Wow, this is amazing, Wai Gong. The goddess is really here. What is it that you want, oh Divine One?" I asked.

Tyler was trying not to laugh.

Chi coughed a couple of times, then stood up tall. "Dearest loyal follower, you have been such a cool old man . . ." I gave her a little kick in the ankle. Deities didn't talk like that!

"Ow, that hurt!" She gave me the evil eye.

"I think you should tell Wai Gong why you have come down from the heavenly realm," I said.

"I was getting to that part, Lizzie."

Wai Gong clapped his hands. "She knows your name, Lizzie! That is such a great honor."

"As I was saying before I was rudely interrupted by this lowly minion . . ." Chi waved her hands around like a magician. I half expected a white rabbit to appear from thin air. "You, Mr. Chu, are going to go on a trip to the Blackpool Tower Ballroom with me and our young friends here. It's what your late wife wanted, and there's someone else who really badly wants you to go. The end."

"Oscar-worthy," mumbled Tyler, laughing into his hands.

"Wai Gong, you said you wouldn't go to Blackpool," I said. "But what if Guan Yin comes with us? She really wants us to go. Don't you, Guan Yin?"

"I do indeed, esteemed Mr. Chu. It was your wife's last wish for you and Lizzie to have the best of times at Blackpool Tower. I command you. Well, not command you—that's not the right word. I really want you to go, basically, and do this nice thing for yourself," said Chi.

I laughed, and Tyler slapped his forehead with his palm.

I took Wai Gong's hand and looked him in the eyes. "Will you change your mind and come with us?" Everything else was in place; I just needed a yes from my grandad. I held my breath, waiting for an answer.

Wai Gong looked delighted, like he had swallowed a cup of "love and light," which was a phrase Tay sometimes said. "Of course, Lizzie. You can't expect me to miss this trip if Guan Yin herself has come to take us. We will be going on our own journey to the west! The Monkey King made the journey with his friends, and Guan Yin watched over them. It's going to be like that." Wai Gong seemed so happy. He looked over to me and smiled. "She's come to look after us."

"Great. I think my dad knows about the journey to the west," Chi said, not knowing she was a character in *The Journey to the West*, the most famous Chinese novel ever written.

"Yes, you are *in* it, Guan Yin," I said, reminding the goddess that she was indeed a very famous deity across the Far East.

Tyler looked at Chi and then at Wai Gong. He gave me a little smile. "He looks really happy," he whispered to me.

I watched as Wai Gong began chattering away to our own Glaswegian-Vietnamese-Welsh Guan Yin. He was showing her his CD collection. Chi was being sweet by nodding a lot and pretending she was interested in his music.

It took us half an hour to get Chi out of Wai Gong's room, as he insisted on telling her about how he used to climb over his neighbor's fence to steal apples when he was a boy.

"Am I doing the right thing, Ty?" I asked. "I know this is really over the top, but I just want to make him happy."

"What can go wrong? We'll take him to Blackpool, he'll have a good time, we'll have a good time, and then we'll bring him back. It's just one day, right?" Tyler said.

Later, as I escorted the goddess out of the flat with Tyler, I gave Chi's wrist a little squeeze to say thank you. I could tell she was loving all the attention, especially when she had to walk down Dumbarton Road dressed in her flowing robes. A car honked its horn as it passed, and Chi waved her hands in the air.

"Goddess in the house! That's right!" she laughed.

I felt so lucky to have two such amazing friends.

"Thanks, guys!" I shouted down the road.

PART TWO

CHAPTER EIGHTEEN

The Mini Orange

It was finally the Sunday we had been waiting for. The day had arrived. My phone alarm woke me at six. We weren't leaving until eight, but I wanted everything to be perfect. I jumped out of bed and opened the curtains. I turned on the water heater. I hadn't had a shower in a few days to save on the bill. The street below was empty apart from a truck collecting the recycling.

I unplugged my phone from the charger. This was my last chance to practice the cha-cha basics. I heard Wai Gong moving about the flat. He was humming to himself, and I could smell toast.

I stood up tall in my pajamas in front of my phone. Smiley Brian from New York appeared on the screen. I must have watched this video a hundred times, though I'd stopped counting. I did the steps along with Brian and Nancy, and for the first time, I felt like I knew what I was doing. Those sneaky dance lessons in between class, chores, and homework these past few weeks had paid off. Only Tyler had seen my moves, as I wanted to surprise Wai Gong and Chi.

"Thanks, Brian and Nancy!" I told the phone screen. "You've been great." It was surprising what you could learn for free from the internet! And even though the lady from Step by Step would never see me dance, I felt like I was getting my own kind of revenge by not giving up and letting her mean words put me off my goal.

I quickly had a shower and got dressed. I put on my black jeans and grey sweatshirt that said NOT CRAZY, NOT RICH, SIMPLY ASIAN and my socks that had dogs on them. I slipped a plain black top in my bag for later, which I'd ironed.

I put the four tickets into my wallet, tucked the envelope full of money into my bag, and had one last look in the mirror. Something was missing. I looked on my dressing table for the jade pendant Grandma Kam had given me for my birthday. It had been my lucky charm for the past few weeks. Now I couldn't find it. But I didn't have time to look. We needed to get ready and on the road.

I was so excited to finally be going somewhere—out of Glasgow, away from this flat, away from cleaning and cooking. I was going to have some fun.

I knocked on Wai Gong's door. "Come in!" he said.

I opened his door. He was dressed and sitting on his bed, putting his socks on.

"You look brilliant, Wai Gong," I told him. He'd even slicked back his hair with some gel.

"I feel good today, Lizzie," he told me. "I can't wait to go."

The buzzer sounded, and I ran to the hallway to pick up the intercom phone.

"Let me in!" Chi squealed. I buzzed her into the downstairs hall, then opened our front door. When I saw Chi, my heart exploded. She was a sight to behold. It really was Guan Yin herself!

Chi and Tyler had outdone themselves with the costume, makeup, and hairpieces. The gold brooch sparkled brightly on top of Chi's head; the white veil cascaded down her back. Her black hair was thick and lustrous. I stood there wide-eyed with my mouth open. The colorful pastel ribbons Tyler had added to Chi's costume made her look ethereal, like she really had come from some heavenly realm rather than Partick in the West End of Glasgow. She looked magical.

"La la la la! One goddess, at your service," Chi said. I laughed.

I grabbed her and gave her the biggest hug. "You look amazing!" I blurted out. "I can't *believe* how good you look."

"What do you mean, you can't believe it? I've got skillz, man," Chi said, laughing.

Just then, Wai Gong came out of his room. He was as starstruck as I was when he saw his beloved goddess manifested in our dingy hallway. He tottered forward, his hands on his chest like he was keeping his heart inside.

"Ohhhh, she's here again! Guan Yin has blessed us again with her presence for this special journey. We must be a blessed family to have the goddess show up for my relative and again for us, Lizzie. It's a sign that things are going to get better. You'll see."

"Ahhh, Mr. Chu, my coolest stan and worshipper guy! I'm ready for the trip to Blackpool. Our chariot awaits us outside. But don't expect that because I'm a goddess I was able to magic up a good ride. It's gonna be tight in that Mini, let me tell ya," Chi said.

"It'll be fine," I told her. "Are we ready to go?" I looked at Wai Gong. He looked so dapper in his suit and tie. He'd even polished his old dance shoes. He wrapped the red scarf around his neck, and he was ready.

"Lizzie, I am so happy we are going to Blackpool Tower Ballroom. The goddess has come to help us make this dream a reality. I am forever grateful to her. I think after this trip, things might be different for us both," Wai Gong said. "I have a feeling. I don't know exactly what is going to happen to us, but it feels like something is changing."

I smiled. "Me too. I think something will change. I think we needed to do something different, Wai Gong. We've been stuck for a long time, haven't we?"

"Stuck no more. We will have a lot of fun."

Downstairs, Tyler and Minh were waiting for us. The Mini Orange looked a lot smaller than I remembered. And rustier too. One of the doors was not orange but blue. And on top of the radio antenna was a Mickey Mouse head with one ear missing.

"Come, Goddess, we're going to ride in this orange car," Wai Gong said, leading Chi to the Mini Orange.

"What took you so long?" Minh asked Chi.

"Speak to the goddess hand," Chi said, putting her palm up in front of her brother's unamused face.

"You know how long it took her to get ready this morning?" Minh asked me. Before I could venture a guess, he blurted out, "Too long!"

"But I look great, don't I?" said Chi, winking at me. I laughed and walked around to the back of the car, hoping to put my bag in the trunk.

"Tyler's already put his huge rucksack in there, so there isn't much room now. You'll have to hold your bag on your lap, Lizzie. Is that okay?" Minh said.

"Okay, that's no problem."

"Do you want to sit in the front, Mr. Chu?" he asked Wai Gong.

"No! I want to sit next to the goddess," he said, climbing into the teeny back seat. Chi smiled and got in next to him.

Her headgear kept getting in the way and bashing the top of the car. Tyler pulled a face and slid into the small space that was left.

"Er . . . she's gone from being a princess to a goddess now? Why's he calling her that?" Minh asked.

"My gramps just likes to call her Goddess. It's a little inside joke they've got going," I said.

"She'll want to be the queen of England next." Minh pinched the top of his nose and didn't look as calm as he normally did. "She looks like one of our bà nội's statues back in Vietnam." I didn't want to reveal that her costume was modeled after that exact statue.

It wasn't going to be a very comfortable trip, from the looks of it. More than three hours squashed like sardines, but it was going to be worth it!

"Why is everyone bringing so much stuff?" Minh asked, a little exasperated. "We're literally just going for one day." He investigated the back seat. Chi was moving about, trying to get comfortable. Wai Gong had his face squashed against the window. He turned and smiled at me.

"Minh! Are we going or what?" Chi shouted.

"All right, then. I just don't get why she's got to dress up like that if it's not a Comic Con—"

"Just relax. Breathe, like your dad would say. Let's go!" I told him.

"Can you film some footage in the car with my phone for my documentary?" he asked.

"Sure."

I got into the passenger seat. Minh got into the driver's seat and handed me his phone. Then he started the car. It spluttered a little before the engine began to hum.

"Blackpool, here we come!" I said.

"Everyone got their seat belts on?" Minh asked.

"Everything is A-OK!" Wai Gong said, grinning.

This was it. The beginning of a new chapter.

CHAPTER NINETEEN

Journey to the West

As the Mini chugged out of the city and along the highway, I looked out the window and smiled. The car didn't have satellite radio or even a CD player, so Minh connected his phone to a portable speaker so we could have some tunes.

Wai Gong was getting into the music. I could see Minh's seat rocking slightly.

"Mr. Chu, can you please stop tapping my chair with your foot when I'm driving?" Minh asked. I could tell he was already annoyed with us all, and we'd only just started the journey.

"Sorry, driver, sorry! How about I tell you all a story? How about *The Journey to the West*—you know, with the Monkey King? It's just like this trip we are on. Guan Yin, do you want to tell it, or shall I?" Wai Gong said.

"You go ahead," said Minh. "I think Bà Nội told us some stories about the Monkey King when we were younger." Minh turned slightly toward Chi. "The Vietnamese have a lot of the same stories and deities as the Chinese. I think it's to do with colonialism and the mixing of cultures that happens over time."

I thought that was interesting.

"Mum always took us to the library when we were little. But we didn't hear many Vietnamese stories from Dad," Chi said.

I turned in my seat so I could see her. She was already looking hot and uncomfortable, beads of sweat dripping down her face. She shifted her body a little to try to get into a better position.

"Go on, Mr. Chu, please tell us the story of the journey," Tyler said.

I hadn't heard this story in such a long time.

Wai Gong rubbed his hands together, excited to begin. Minh was trying to concentrate on the road. The car was vrooming along at sixty miles per hour behind a large truck.

"*The Journey to the West* is very long, so I will tell you my favorite bits," Wai Gong said. "It was written by Wu Cheng'en and is one of the most famous Chinese stories of all time. Let's begin."

The Journey to the West

The monk Tripitaka had to recover the lost Buddhist scriptures from India by taking the Silk Road. Guan Yin, my beloved goddess of compassion and mercy, took it upon herself to oversee the mission. She found him three companions.

Sun Wukong, also called the Monkey King, was known for his mischievous and selfish nature. When the goddess found him, he was trapped under a mountain. In return for his freedom, Guan Yin offered him the chance to go on the mission and protect the monk. Next was Zhu Bajie, known as Pigsy because of his piglike appearance. He loved eating and sleeping. The third pilgrim, Sha Wujing, was known as Sandy. He was strong and was said to be part fish, part ogre.

They made their way along a mountain path and faced many obstacles. Their first stop was at an abbey. Tripitaka did not want to eat, but the Monkey King decided they should try the magic fruits. While gathering the fruit, they accidentally cut the magical tree. They were all in big trouble. Monkey flew to see Guan Yin and asked her to help. She flew to the abbey and restored the magic tree to its former glory.

On the next mountain, a zombie called White Lady Bone was waiting for them. She wanted to eat Tripitaka, as the monk's flesh was holy. She tried to trick the pilgrims by disguising herself. But Monkey was uneasy—he could sense evil in the area. He was quick to defeat her with his staff.

Later, a sorcerer turned Tripitaka into a tiger and was going to eat him. When Monkey arrived to save Tripitaka, he declared, "I am the Monkey King!" The sorcerer knew of the Monkey King's reputation and was afraid of him. He surrendered and turned Tripitaka back to his human form.

And on they went. More obstacles and demons crossed their path, but the pilgrims carried on and each grew to understand himself better. They reached their destination and returned with the sacred scrolls. Guan Yin was pleased with their progress, and their reward was enlightenment!

When Wai Gong finished, Tyler and Chi erupted into a round of applause. I'd heard the story a thousand times, but it was great to hear it again and for my friends to hear it too.

"That was fantastic, Mr. Chu," said Tyler. "All those demons!"

"And zombies!" said Chi.

"Guan Yin could have magicked them all the way to India on a floating cloud," I said. "She had the power to, yet she chose not to."

"Yes, the monk and his companions had to make the journey to learn something about themselves," Chi said. "And I gave them enlightenment. See how cool I am?"

We all laughed.

Wai Gong nodded in delight. "Exactly! I am like the monk, wise and old," he said. "A little bit naughty too!"

"Oooh, can I be the Monkey King?" Minh said, joining in. "I wish I could fly around on clouds like he does. And if I had that magic staff, I would be the boss man."

"This car is just like one of the magic clouds," Tyler said.

I wasn't so sure about that! It was starting to make a weird rattling sound.

"As long as no one says I'm Pigsy!" I said. "We have our very own Guan Yin here." I turned around. Chi gave a little bow of her head. She was scrolling on her phone.

"Yeah, right," said Minh. "She's more like that zombie demon woman."

"Hey! Watch it, Minh Pham!" Chi said.

"I want to be Pigsy," said Tyler, pushing the tip of his nose into the air with his finger. "I like eating food and sleeping. I'd be perfect."

"Lizzie can be Sandy. Quiet and strong, but when you get on her nerves, she will eat you like an ogre! Ha ha!" Wai Gong said. "She killed a dead chicken the other day!"

"Wai Gong, it was already dead. I just sort of . . . got it run over!" I laughed. It felt good to relax and not have to worry about whether we had enough food in the house or whether Wai Gong was happy. He was clearly very happy.

"Lizzie, don't worry. You're not Sandy," said Chi, looking at her phone. "It says on this website that Sandy was a fish ogre with matted hair and a necklace of skulls—sounds just like Minh to me. I don't know why girls gush over him all the time. He definitely seems more like Sandy to me." She laughed.

"You're just jealous, sprout. What is the moral of the story, Mr. Chu?" asked Minh. "Was Monkey meant to learn a lesson from the trip?"

But instead of Wai Gong answering, Chi piped up. "They all did. The story shows that even though a journey may not always go the way you expect, it might be the way you need."

I'd never heard anything so profound come out of Chi's mouth before. Even Tyler was shocked. Minh looked at me and raised his eyebrows.

"The goddess is right. It's about the journey, not the destination. About personal growth," Wai Gong said.

I looked out my window. I saw fields upon fields. It was so good to be out of the city, to be with friends and Wai Gong. I rolled down the window slightly, and a rush of wind hit the side of my face; I put my fingers up to feel the breeze. I could sense how the journey was already making us feel different about ourselves. I'd learned a little basic cha-cha, and Tyler was going to see the sea for the first time. Chi was being a goddess for the day, and Minh would get footage for his film project. And Wai Gong . . . well, he was already acting more upbeat than he had in months. I was excited to see where this journey would take us.

A grating sound started to hurt my ears, so I rolled up the window. It must have been the wind.

We drove on for another hour. Minh told us the story of the Vietnamese Cinderella, "Tam and Cam," which his grandmother had told him when he had visited her in Hanoi a few years ago.

Chi was doing well being the goddess in the back seat. She tried not to give definitive answers to any of Wai Gong's questions. There was a lot of "it shall be so" and "this is the way," which I was sure she had lifted from *The Mandalorian*. She was loving being someone else for a day. Minh rolled his eyes.

"Lizzie, is Chi okay? She's acting all nice with your grandad. She's not usually like that."

"Yeah, she's fine. It's the outfit. It's made her much nicer to be around," I said.

"Bizarro," said Minh, none the wiser.

"How much longer until we get there? I don't think I can sit in this position for much longer. I need to stretch my legs," Tyler said, taking out his water bottle and drinking a large swig.

"I was hoping to drive all the way there without stopping," Minh said.

Tyler let out a humongous burp. Everyone was silent, and then we all burst out laughing. Everyone except Minh, who had both hands tightly on the wheel. There was a noise coming from somewhere, and it wasn't the wind. He slowed the car down a little and moved to the left lane. Something was not right. The car began to make stranger chugging noises.

"This is definitely not divine. I think our journey to the west is going to be just like the story—now the demons are coming," said Wai Gong as white smoke began pouring from the hood. *The demons have caught up with us for sure,* I thought.

CHAPTER TWENTY

Sidetracked

"No . . . no . . . no!" Minh said as the car began to move as if it were coughing. It jerked forward, spluttering like someone with a bad cold.

"Guan Yin, bless us, this does not look good," Wai Gong said.

"Dad told you not to use your pal for the emissions test, Minh! You should have listened to him!" Chi yelled.

"I don't need to hear that from you right now, Goddess!" Minh yelled, banging his hands on the steering wheel.

"We're not going to make it," Tyler said.

"Shhhhhh!" I said. I didn't need him making the argument worse.

"The engine is overheating," said Minh. "I shouldn't have said yes to driving you. The car hasn't been on a trip this long before. I knew this was a bad idea!" Plumes of smoke rose into the sky.

"Come on, Guan Yin, you can save us," said Wai Gong. "Like the time you helped Monkey in *The Journey to the West*. Remember? You can make the car fly because you are a goddess."

"Everyone, get into brace position. I've seen this on TV for when a plane might crash," Chi said. I turned to see her bracing herself and trying to put her head down, but the brooch and hairpieces wouldn't allow her to bend over properly.

"What's she talking about?" Minh asked. "I don't need this, Lizzie . . . I have to stop the car." Minh was panicking. We heard a loud horn behind us, and the smoke was getting so bad we could hardly see through the front window.

I held on to the dashboard in front of me. Tyler squeezed my shoulder. The horn blared longer and longer. Something was very close behind us. It felt big—I could feel the shadow gaining on us—and Tyler's fingers squeezed tighter. Cars were putting on their hazard lights to warn us, but we couldn't see what was going on.

"Lizzie, press the hazard light button—it's a triangle, I think," Minh said, concentrating on not hitting a black SUV.

I started pressing all the buttons on the dashboard.

"No, not those . . . over to the left. Why did I agree to this?" Minh lamented.

I accidentally turned on the radio. An old song came on at full volume. It was about monsters mashing or something.

"I love this song." Wai Gong started to clap his hands.

I scrambled around trying to turn it off. Minh was huffing and banging buttons, and all the while, the truck honking at us was getting even closer.

"I'm too young to die, and I can't die in this outfit!" Chi yelped as the car began to judder and splutter.

"Everything will be okay because *you* are here," Wai Gong said, quite unaffected by the fact that the car could be squashed like a fly at any moment.

Minh swerved over to the shoulder and jammed his foot down on the brake. The huge truck roared past, shaking the little Mini like a maraca, and then we came to a complete stop.

Minh slammed his hands down on the wheel. I thought he was going to bang his head on it too. But thankfully he didn't. I could see his chest rising and falling very fast.

"Perfect, just perfect!" he exclaimed.

I turned around and looked at everyone. Chi was sobbing into her hands. Black mascara was dripping onto her outfit. Tyler was flapping a Kleenex about, trying to wipe black marks from Chi's robe. She kept batting his hands away. Wai Gong was frowning while looking out the window.

"Why are we not moving?" Wai Gong said. "We will still be able to go, right, Goddess? You can do something to help us?"

Chi shrugged and sniffed, wiping her face on her sleeve.

"You're getting the robe all dirty, Chi! Stop crying. I worked hard on that. You'll look like Cruella de Vil!" Tyler tried to lift Chi's head up. I found a packet of tissues in my bag and gave her one, then turned back to look at Minh. He was pinching the bridge of his nose again.

I took a deep breath. "It's a minor setback," I told Chi, not really believing what I was saying.

"I thought this was going to be fun," she complained. "Lizzie, this was a bad idea."

"No, it's *got* to work. It's our mission. We can't give up now," I said. I sighed the biggest sigh.

"We will make it, won't we, Guan Yin?" asked Wai Gong. "You know how important this is to Lizzie and me. We have to get to the Blackpool Tower Ballroom for afternoon tea, or afternoon cha." He patted Minh on the back. "You know the word for tea in Chinese sounds like cha-cha, the dance?"

Minh had clearly had enough. He opened his car door and got out. He bent down and looked at us one at a time through the open doorway.

"Everyone, please get out and go to the grassy bit over there," said Minh. "I'll call Mum and Dad to come and get us."

"No, wait!" I urged, opening my door and going round to where Minh was standing. "Please don't. We're more than half-way there. We can get the car fixed and still spend the day in

Blackpool. We can get a tow truck to take us there and then drive us all home."

"No, Lizzie. It's not going to happen. Everyone out!"

Wai Gong, Chi, and Tyler got out of the car.

Minh pulled out his phone. "Mum is going to tell me she knew it was a bad idea to buy this car. 'I told you so' is what she's going to say. I hate those 'I told you so' speeches."

The highway traffic was roaring past; Wai Gong held his hands over his ears. Chi had stopped crying, but her face was streaked with black and her lipstick was smeared all over her cheeks. She looked more like a vampire gone wrong than a compassionate goddess. She grabbed my arm and pulled me over to the grass.

"I'm *done* with being the goddess, Lizzie. I just wanna put my leggings on and lie on my bed. This is not what I signed up for. I agree with Minh for once. I think we need to call my parents to come and get us."

"Chi, it's just a minor hiccup. It's like *The Journey to the West*. Monkey and the others had loads of obstacles—demons, even, and that's way worse than this," I said.

"That's just a silly story, Lizzie. This is real life. We're stuck on the side of the highway," Chi said.

"Let's figure this out," I said. "We can't give up! What if we hitched a ride to Blackpool? We can make a sign asking for help. What do you think?"

"Hitch a ride? Have you heard of serial killers?" asked Minh. "I've seen all the documentaries about them." He lifted up the hood, which had stopped producing smoke but was clearly still hot. "Owww! I've no idea what I am looking at." He held his forehead, an expression of despair on his face.

Wai Gong sat on the grass and got out his thermos of hot water. He began to slurp. "This is exactly what happened to Monkey, and Guan Yin helped him out," he said. "It's going to be fine. Just you wait and see. Divine help will come." He opened a Tupperware container, pulled out an orange, and began peeling it. He offered the box to Chi. She sat down next to him and took a couple of grapes. Then Tyler sat down too and opened a bag of potato chips. Minh tapped his phone and then held it in the air at funny angles.

"I can't get a signal here—we're in a reception black spot or something. Just what I don't need. Can you all look and see if you have a signal?" Minh asked.

We all got our phones out.

"Nope, nothing here," Chi said, shoving her phone back into the pocket Tyler had made for her inside the robe.

"I've got one bar of service!" I shouted. I was about to hand my phone to Minh, but then the bar disappeared. "No, now it's gone." I waved my phone in the air, hoping for some luck, but it didn't work.

Tyler did the same, then shook his head.

"What are we going to do?" I asked.

Wai Gong was watching the traffic; he waved as a bus going to Blackpool sped by.

"I'll have to look for an emergency phone along the shoulder. I'm just going down there. Don't move, any of you." Minh stomped off.

We looked like a sorry bunch.

CHAPTER TWENTY-ONE

Vroom!

Minh came back fuming.

"Someone vandalized the emergency telephone, can you believe it?"

"Kids these days," Tyler said. "Sheesh."

Chi was pacing back and forth. I was worried she was going to have a meltdown and then Wai Gong would get nervous too. I looked over at him. He was sitting cross-legged on the grass now and had his eyes closed. Chi pulled Minh away from us and started talking to him in a hushed but angry way. I felt sorry for Minh; I was the one who had dragged him along. The siblings' argument was starting to get really heated.

"This is so bad," I exclaimed to Tyler.

"It's going to get worse," he replied, looking past my shoulder.

Just then, we heard a roar of engines. It was just like thunder, getting closer and closer. We all stood up apart from Wai Gong, who was still resting his eyes. Minh and Chi stopped fighting and came over to where Tyler and I were standing. Chi held my arm tight.

A gang of bikers was slowing down and heading right for us.

"It's those Hairy Bikers or Devil Bikers . . . or whatever they're called," Chi said.

"Hells Angels," said Minh.

"They don't look like angels to me," said Chi as eight broad-shouldered leather-clad figures with dark helmets that covered their whole faces pulled up behind Minh's car. Tyler, Chi, and I took a step back behind Minh.

I gulped. What were they going to do to us? What if they tried to steal the money we'd raised? I knew we had to hide the envelope stuffed with money just in case. I spun around; Tyler was behind me next to the car.

"Hide this, Ty," I said, shoving the envelope into his hand. He looked around in a panic, opened the car door, and shoved the envelope down the side of the back seat.

Minh had his hands on his hips. The rest of us cowered behind him.

The shortest one at the front turned his engine off and got off his bike.

Chi grabbed my arm and pinched it tight. Her fake nails were digging into my flesh. "Oh god, oh god," she said.

All of them parked behind the Mini Orange like their leader, turned their engines off, and sat on their bikes, staring at us. The leader was shorter than me, but he was stocky. His leather jacket had a patch with flames on it. My knees began to give way and I gulped. I imagined a headline in tomorrow's newspaper:

Adolescents and Old Man Stranded on Highway Disappear. Police Suspect Foul Play by Hairy Bikers.

The leader walked over to me.

"How do . . . kids . . . need help?" The voice had a gravelly tone like sandpaper, and I couldn't make out all the words through the motorcycle helmet.

Chi pushed Minh forward. "You talk to them, Minh—you're the designated adult," she said. Minh turned around and gave her the most annoyed look a brother could give his kid sister. Then he faced the biker.

"I've called my parents. They know where we are and they're coming to get us," Minh lied. "And there are CCTV cameras all along the highway."

"They're coming closer, Minh, do something!" Chi shouted.

Tyler grabbed my hand.

The leader took off his helmet—and her long brown hair with a few bits that had turned grey fell down around her ears. It was a woman! She looked around the same age as our head teacher, Mrs. Arnold. She held out a pack of chewing gum. "Fancy a piece?"

The other bikers took off their helmets too. They were *all* women! Some were younger, and others looked around the same age as the leader. One had bright white hair.

"I'm Margaret, but people call me Marge. I'm the leader of the pack. We're Marge's Angels. Nice to meet you young'uns. Looks like you need a hand."

Marge's Angels?

Tyler smiled and took a piece of gum. "We thought you were going to rob us," he said.

"We might look tough, but we're kind lasses," Marge said, amused. "We raised four thousand pounds for the children's hospital last year."

"Do you have any ID?" Chi asked suspiciously. I nudged her in the side. "Lizzie, rule number one when approached by strangers is to ask for ID. Or is it to run away?"

"I think they're all right," I told her.

Marge swiveled around to show us the emblem on her back. The rest of the pack did the same. On their leather jackets were patches with flames on them, and in the center they said MARGE'S ANGELS.

"How's that for ID?" Marge said, facing us once more. "Our names are on our jackets." She showed me a label sewn to the front of hers, which indeed said MARGE. They all turned back to face us, and we began reading their names. "We're the only all-female motorcycle group in this region. Some of us are from Yorkshire, others from Lancashire. We're not going to hurt you!" Marge said, laughing.

"That's so awesome!" said Tyler.

"We thought you might need a lift somewhere. Looks like your car is well and truly dead," said another woman, peeking under the open hood. According to the label on her jacket, she was called Rhonda. She had short black hair with a pink streak in the front, and her tattooed belly was hanging out of her black T-shirt. "I can have a look at it if you want me to. I'm a mechanic." Rhonda got out a few tools from her saddlebag.

Minh nodded and stepped back. Rhonda bent over the front of the car; her head disappeared under the hood. She resurfaced with a smudge of motor oil on her face, which she wiped off with her fingertips.

"This car isn't going anywhere. The alternator belt has broken," Rhonda said.

I saw Minh's expression go from slight worry to full-on panic. "Are you sure?" he asked, trying to see over Rhonda's shoulder.

"Call your roadside recovery service. Your car insurance might be able to help," Marge said.

"Insurance . . . right. My dad sorted that out for me, but I don't have the paperwork here, and I can't get my parents on the phone, as I've got no service," Minh said. "I knew this was a bad idea. If only I could call Dad . . ." Minh started tapping his phone screen like that was going to help at all.

"Yeah, you're in a black spot because of the hills on both sides. You need to get out of this area. There's no mobile service until after the next junction," said a biker whose jacket identified her as Bertha. "We could take them to Violet's?"

"Hmmm..." said Marge, holding her chin. She looked around at her bike and then at us as if calculating something.

I stepped forward, hoping we wouldn't need to abandon the mission. I looked over at Wai Gong, whose eyes were still closed.

"Hi there. I'm Lizzie. We need to get to Blackpool. It's a matter of urgency," I told Marge. "Do you think you can help us?" I had my fingers crossed.

"Maybe on the backs of your bikes?" Tyler asked. I saw him eyeing the bike with red-and-yellow flames on the sides. Trust Tyler to go for the flashy one.

"I'm not sure we should leave the car here," Minh said nervously.

"But we can't stay here for hours waiting for the tow truck or your parents," I said. Tyler nodded, backing me up.

"I dunno, Lizzie," said Chi. "Have you seen this robe I'm wearing? It's whiter than white. If I get on one of those bikes, I'll get oil and who knows what else on it."

"But we don't have many options, and a dirty goddess in Blackpool is better than none of us arriving there at all," I said.

"I guess so," said Chi. "All right, I'm in too."

"We can take you some of the way," said Bertha. "Six of

the lasses have double seats for passengers. We're just on our way to Marge's auntie Violet's for sausage sandwiches for breakfast—she makes her own sausages, you see. The best in Lancashire. There's a train station nearby, which is not that far from Blackpool."

"Oh, that would be perfect!" I shouted in delight. "A ride would be very welcome. Thank you so much." If we could get closer to Blackpool, we'd be all right. We might have less time at the theme park, but we'd still be in time for the Blackpool Tower Ballroom.

"I'm in charge of you all," said Minh. "Mum and Dad would kill me if they knew I'd let you go on motorbikes. You know how protective they are of you, Chi."

"Most of us have got first aid training," said Rhonda. "Not that anything will happen," she added quickly.

"Come on, Minh," Chi said. "We can't sit here all day. Mum would want us to think outside the box, and getting on these bikes would be just that, right?"

Minh nodded. "Yeah, I suppose. I just don't know what to do, really."

Marge looked at Chi from her head to her toes.

"Aren't you a bit young to be getting married, love? Is that why you're all dressed up like that?" asked Marge. "We love a good wedding. Dot married Rhonda last year. We were all bridesmaids and drove behind the wedding car."

"No, I helped make this costume for Chi," said Tyler. "It's a long story. We just want Lizzie and her grandad to get to Blackpool, that's all."

"I love Blackpool—the kids screaming on the rides, the rebel seagulls trying to eat your fish and chips, the smell of dough-nuts and sea salt along the pier," laughed Rhonda, putting her tools away. Rhonda was less scary when she laughed. I saw Minh relax his shoulders. She punched him on the arm. "Come on, we're here to help ya. We're angels, after all."

Marge laughed. "It'll be fun. What do you say, Minh, is it?"

Minh looked at Chi and Tyler and me. Then he looked at Wai Gong, who was still sitting behind us on the grass.

"It's an emergency, Minh," Chi said. She turned to Marge. "Don't go too fast though, okay?"

"It'll be like riding one of the things in *Star Wars*—you know, the ones Leia and Luke ride through the forest of Endor." I always surprised myself with how much *Star Wars* knowledge I had, and now I was thankful it was just enough to convince the superfan to do my bidding.

"All right," said Chi.

Minh nodded. "I guess it's better than sticking around here. Thanks, we'd love a lift."

Tyler ran over to one of the bikes and put on the spare hel-met. He grinned. "I've always wanted to ride on the back of one of these things!"

I grabbed Chi's arm. "Come help me convince Wai Gong to get on the back of one of those bikes."

We ran over to where Wai Gong was sitting. His eyes were now open, and he smiled at us.

"Mr. Chu, our prayers have been answered," said Chi, waving her arms around for effect.

"We're still going to Blackpool, aren't we?" he said. "Who are those people by the car?"

"Really nice ladies. We've got a new ride! You must hold on to one of those ladies tightly." I pointed to the bikers. "Guan Yin, can you tell him it's going to be okay?"

"Yes, that's me, Guan Yin . . . right, I need to say something now, don't I? We should go with them. Lizzie is right," Chi said.

"Are you sure it's okay to go with them?" Wai Gong asked as we started to walk toward the bikers.

I watched as Tyler opened the trunk to get his huge rucksack. Then Minh got out his camera bag and grabbed my bag from the front seat. He handed it to Rhonda, who gave me a thumbs-up. She was going to be my ride.

"Mr. Chu, these biker ladies are going to take us closer to Blackpool. It's our only way out of this mess," Chi said.

"Thanks, Goddess," I said, taking Wai Gong to his metal steed and rider, Bertha. Bertha was silent and didn't smile. She grunted. Then she handed Wai Gong a helmet, which had brown bear ears sticking out of the top. He put it on. I wanted to laugh out loud, but Wai Gong was looking a little nervous.

He nodded to Bertha, who revved her engine. The sound was loud. Wai Gong looked at me and gingerly climbed onto the back of Bertha's bike, which said THE BEAST along the side.

"Is this really okay, Lizzie? Goddess?" he asked.

"Sure, it's just like *The Journey to the West*," said Chi. "Many obstacles got in the way of Monk Tripitaka and the rest of them on their journey to India, but Guan Yin was always there . . . and I'll be there when we reach the town." She patted his arm reassuringly.

Wai Gong was about to reply when Bertha kicked up the bike stand, and they drove away before any of us could say another word.

"Ready?" asked Rhonda. She handed me my bag and a helmet with a sticker on it that read BIKER GALS RULE.

"Ready!" I said, grinning.

Minh, Chi, and Tyler got onto their rides, and I saw Minh look lovingly at the Mini Orange. I hoped the car would be okay. The bikers gave thumbs-up, and the engines roared.

Off we sped! I felt a jolt of excitement in my belly as I held tight to Rhonda's waist.

Blackpool, here we come. Again!

CHAPTER TWENTY-TWO

The Best Sausage Sandwich in Lancashire (and the World)

My butt was a little sore from sitting on the back of a motor-cycle for forty minutes. But it was so much fun, the wind lashing my face as I watched the landscape rush by. My thighs were aching a little from holding on so tight.

Wai Gong had his hands in the air like he was on a roller coaster. Bertha kept patting him on the thigh to remind him not to let go. The bottom of Chi's robe was fluttering about in the wind. She looked like a ghost on a motorbike.

Marge's Angels took us to a small village on the outskirts of Bamber Bridge, then to a little greasy spoon café on the main street called the Hot Bite. The motorbikes all pulled up, and we got off. Tyler was rubbing his behind. Wai Gong was chatting to Bertha.

"Thank you so much for the fantastic ride. You are the most esteemed biker I have ever met! This was truly fate. The young ones think it's all chance, you know . . . but the goddess is giving me a lot of good luck lately."

Bertha laughed. "No problem, mate. Wait until you try Violet's sausage sandwiches. That'll make your day for sure!" She opened the worn green door of the café.

Wai Gong began to sniff the air. "What is that *smell?*" he asked.

"I told you! Violet's sausages are the best in the whole northeast. It's her husband who's a pig farmer, but she adds some special ingredient," said Chi's biker, who was just a bit older than Mrs. Begum from the looks of it. Not young enough to go clubbing, but not old enough to wear old-fashioned clothes yet. Her bike had a black-and-pink striped theme going on.

Minh got off his bike with his camera bag. Chi was looking particularly disheveled—there were black oil stains on the bottom of her robe, and her hairpieces were falling all over her face. Wai Gong didn't seem to notice; he took her by the arm, smiling.

"Ahh, you really are looking after me—thank you."

"Sure I am. I'm going to stuff my face with a sausage and ketchup sandwich, and then I'll feel better. That ride made my belly feel all funny," Chi said.

"But you're a being who does not eat animals," Wai Gong said, confused.

"Today, I eat *all* the animals. I deserve to eat all the animals, and I will eat all the animals. It's not easy being a goddess. Where are the sausage sandwiches? I need one now!" Chi said.

She stomped into the café after the bikers. She sat down, adjusted the front part of her hairpiece—the brooch had fallen over one eye—and puffed her hair back up. Then she ordered a sandwich from Violet, who was a very short, round lady with bright purple hair. She had thick red glasses that matched her red lipstick.

"Hey! You brought me a lot of new customers, Margey!" shouted Violet as her niece poured herself a cup of tea behind the counter.

"We rescued them from the shoulder of the highway. They're from Glasgow, but they need to get to Blackpool," Marge said.

"We could all come and visit you, try one of those deep-fried Mars bars from Glasgow I keep hearing about," Violet said.

"Or you could come to our café—Soya Bean Café—and try some of my mum's tofu," Minh said.

"Get the deep-fried Mars bar," Chi said.

Tyler, Minh, and I sat down at a wooden table. The bikers took off their leather jackets and hung them up. They were quite a varied bunch, all different shapes and sizes.

"Thanks for getting us this far," I said to Marge. "It really means a lot that you rescued us."

"No problem, love, it was our pleasure. Let us get you some food—you all look hungry. Then you can check the train schedule."

"This is great," said Minh. "Lady bikers rescuing a bunch of kids and an old man—that's actually a really good story." He got out his camera and began going around asking the bikers if he could film them. They all loved it. They puffed up their flattened hair, and Marge put on some fuchsia lip gloss.

"I've always fancied myself an actress," said Marge. "I love those Agatha Christie whodunits. And *Murder, She Wrote!*" She and Minh sat down in the corner, and he started to ask her questions.

I turned my attention to Chi, who was being very quiet. "Chi, are you okay?" I asked as Violet placed two sausage sandwiches before the disheveled goddess. "Are you hungry, then? Two sandwiches?"

"Starving, I'm absolutely starving. More than you could know. You know I eat when I get stressed," she said. She started to eat as if she hadn't eaten in a week. Drops of ketchup dribbled down her chin. The vegan goddess was not a vegan today!

My belly began to make gurgling noises—I'd skipped breakfast, as I was too nervous and excited about the trip. Violet brought me a sandwich too. I took a bite, and it was true: This was the best sausage sandwich I had ever tasted.

"Thanks, this is delicious!" I said between bites.

"Oh! I needed that. This is literally the best food that has passed my lips in all my life!" Chi said, looking the perkiest I had seen her all day. "Breaking down was worth it to taste that!"

I nodded in agreement. Violet's sausage sandwiches were amazing, and I now understood why the bikers rode all the way out here to eat them.

"So how often do you all go out together?" Minh asked, filming Marge with his small handheld camera.

"Once a month, usually. We've never rescued stranded kids on the shoulder before though. What are you doing in Blackpool?" she asked.

"It's Lizzie's idea," interrupted Chi. She lowered her voice so Wai Gong couldn't hear. "We're on a journey to the west—or Blackpool, rather—because her dead gran got us tickets to the Tower. It's a long story. Once she gets a thought into her head, she has to follow through."

Tyler stepped forward and added, "She learned the cha-cha so she can dance it with her gramps. Blackpool Tower Ballroom is where he met her grandma. It was her grandma's last wish that they go there again."

"Ahhhhh," came a chorus from the bikers.

I blushed.

The bikers were all getting teary-eyed.

"Sounds like a lovely idea," said Marge. "Blackpool is great fun, especially for ballroom dancing fans, although it's more run-down than it used to be. You must be the best granddaughter."

"I try. It's not always easy now that it's just the two of us," I told her.

Wai Gong was walking around the café looking at photos of the biker ladies on the wall. Minh was fiddling with a lens on his fancy camera.

"And why are you filming?" Marge asked him.

"I'm doing a film course, and I have to hand in a documentary, so I thought I would film this story about a young carer who's desperate to take her grandad to Blackpool. It's like an issues piece."

"What did you call me?" I asked. "A young carer?" I hadn't been called a carer before. I wasn't sure I liked the sound of it.

"It's what it sounds like, Lizzie. A young person who has caring responsibilities. That's you," Minh said. "It means you've taken on tasks adults usually do around the house."

I frowned.

"Why are you looking at me like that?" Minh asked.

"I don't like being called that. I'm not a young anything." Putting a label on what I did made it seem strange. And "young" made it seem like I wasn't up to the job.

"I work in a care home, and being a carer is not easy. Having that amount of responsibility at your age is a lot. You should be out playing and having a good time with your mates," Marge said.

"It's not a bad thing, Lizzie, to be called a carer. And you can get some help if you want it. I've said this before. My aunt is a social worker. She can help you out," Tyler said.

I felt like I was being bombarded suddenly from all directions—first Minh, then Marge, and now Tyler.

"A carer! Oof, that's difficult enough for an adult, never mind a young lass like yourself," said Dot, a burly biker with a red bandana around her head. "I looked after my mum for a few years—she had Alzheimer's, which is a type of dementia. We didn't realize at first, but then the forgetting began, and one day I visited and she'd forgotten who I was, just like that. It's a lot for a young girl."

"What kind of forgetting?" Tyler asked.

"She sometimes thought she was a young girl again. She remembered games she'd played as a kid but couldn't remember if her shopping had been delivered that day. Things like that. When she was bad, she mistook me for my auntie Barb, who was long dead. It was sad." Then Dot added, "You're only young, you shouldn't have that burden, love."

Rhonda came over and put her arm around Dot's shoulders.

"Honestly, I'm fine." I looked over at Wai Gong, "We're fine. We don't need anyone's help. I just do the shopping, that's all."

"You do more than that, Lizzie," said Tyler. The bikers were all listening now. Wai Gong had gone into the kitchen with Violet to see where she cooked her famous sausages. "You clean, and you sort out all the bills. Your grandad missed parents' evening again. You're always worried about him."

"And tell them about that time you had to get food from the church," said Chi.

"Chi! You said you wouldn't tell anyone about that," I said.

Suddenly, I felt guilty about everything. Why was everyone looking at me? Everyone seemed to have an opinion about my life.

"Your grandad doesn't do any of those things?" Marge asked. "Not even pay the bills?"

I shook my head.

"He wanders around a lot, doesn't he, Lizzie?" Chi said. "He's always out."

"No, he's been looking for part-time work. That's why he's out a lot." I knew that wasn't exactly the truth. I took a deep breath and thought about how he had been acting lately: the lost keys that weren't lost, his turning up at Comic Con and thinking Chi was a goddess. Was it more than just grief? Something about what Dot had said was making me feel strange. I looked down at the floor.

"Let's ... let's talk about something else. It's a lot to take in," said Tyler. He put his arm around me and squeezed my shoulders. Little did we know that things were about to get even more complicated.

CHAPTER TWENTY-THREE

A Quick Exit

"Let's talk about your costume instead," Bertha said, looking at Chi, who stood out like a sore thumb among the black-clad bikers. She'd been pretty quiet up until now.

"Why don't you guess why I'm dressed like this?" Chi said, relishing the attention. "You will never get it!"

Marge took in Chi from head to toe. "Oh, I love a good mystery to solve!" she said, clapping her hands together.

"You're going to Holy Communion?" Bertha said.

Chi shook her head.

"No, she's dressed like one of her favorite film characters. You know the young'uns love that stuff these days. My niece is into anime," Rhonda said.

"You're a fairy or a princess in a theater show?" Marge guessed.

Chi laughed and shook her head.

"Good guess though," said Tyler.

"Shall we tell them why I'm really dressed up like this, Lizzie?" Chi asked.

I shook my head. I didn't think it was the right time.

"I think it's okay to let everyone know, Lizzie," Tyler said.

"My little sister likes to dress up and be the center of attention," Minh said. "Isn't that right, sprout? You're all about you."

My hands started to get sweaty.

Chi glared at Minh. "I'm not selfish, and I'm dressed like this to help Lizzie and her grandad. I'm being compassionate, if you don't mind." She folded her arms and pouted.

Minh was being particularly hard on Chi, and I needed to set the record straight. Chi often stuck up for Tyler and me, and now it was my turn to return the favor.

"Chi's telling the truth. She's not doing it to be the center of attention. She's helping out her best mate. It was my idea. My grandad loves this Chinese deity called Guan Yin. She's loved around the world. Chi's dressed as her," I said. "I asked her to be a goddess for a day."

"Oh yeah, now I see it. I think I've seen pictures of that goddess before when I visited my gran in Vietnam," said Minh. "But why? I still don't get it."

"It started the day of Comic Con, when I was dressed as Princess Leia," said Chi. "I had the hood on, remember? When Mr. Chu saw me, he thought I looked like Guan Yin. But he actually believes I *am* her."

Minh turned around and lowered the camera to face the floor. "Did you say Mr. Chu thinks you really are the goddess in the story he told?"

"Yes, that's right," I said. "He didn't want to come to Blackpool because he thought it was bad luck that he'd broken his Guan Yin statue—he was keeping the tickets safe under it. So I needed Chi to persuade him to come." I felt bad now that I was explaining it to everyone. It sounded ridiculous.

"Her grandad only listens to me," Chi said.

"This is way too surreal. And wrong," said Minh. "We're taking someone who could be sick and needs help on a road trip. Lizzie, you have some explaining to do. I would never have agreed to this if I'd known the truth."

"Wai Gong is fine apart from the goddess thing," I insisted. "But that's why this trip is so important. It will reset him like a clock. He's just sad because of Grandma Kam dying. I'm sorry, Minh. I really needed you to drive us, so I didn't want to tell you. I wanted to make him happy, that's all."

"So you all tricked me into coming—not cool. Not cool. Wait until I tell Mum and Dad," Minh said. "I'm going to call them right now to come and get us."

"But she's on her journey, her mission, Minh. Lizzie needs this as well as her grandad," Tyler said.

"You can't end the trip. I need to take him there!" I said. "I'm sorry we didn't tell you everything. I've just been . . . well . . .

scared about things changing. He's the only family I've got. We've come so far, Minh."

"It's one day out. Let's just have a good time?" Chi said.

"I'm going out front to call my parents. The best thing to do is go back home, Lizzie. I'm sorry this hasn't worked out," Minh said. He left the table and went outside. The bikers began clearing up the plates.

"Lizzie? Are you okay? You look a bit . . . pale," Tyler said.

"This is all I have right now, Tyler. This trip." I could feel the tears welling up in my eyes. Our own journey to the west was on the brink of failing.

"You've got us," said Chi, patting my hand. She bent over and whispered into my ear, "If I were the goddess, which I am, I'd say we still could get you and your gramps to the Tower Ballroom on time. Come on—we'll leave Minh here and sneak out the back. If he wants to stay and be picked up, then that's up to him."

"I don't know what you are whispering, but I am in!" Tyler said, his face lit up. He was up for more adventure. He grabbed his bag from under the table.

"Marge, how often do the trains run to Blackpool from here?" Chi asked.

I beamed at my besties; they didn't want to give up. I gave Tyler a look of thanks, and I put my hands on Chi's wrist to let her know I was eternally grateful.

169

"They're on the hour. You'd have to run, but you could make the next one. The station is only five minutes away."

"Right, we'll get your gramps and sneak out the back," Chi said.

The bikers were smiling.

"We'll look after Minh. You get to Blackpool," said Rhonda.

"Tyler, give me the money envelope so I can pay for the sandwiches before we go," I said.

Tyler rummaged around in his rucksack. He looked up with an expression I did not want to see. "It's not here . . . it's not in my rucksack . . ."

My stomach lurched. I'd given Tyler the envelope when I was panicking by the highway. "What do you mean, it's not there?"

"It's in the car. I hid it because we thought we were going to be robbed by the bikers," Tyler reminded us.

"We have no money?" Chi said. "Just great. How could this day get any worse?"

"Don't worry about the sandwiches—they're on the house," said Violet, coming back in and wiping her hands on her pink apron. "This gentleman has been entertaining me with stories of Chinese mythology for the past five minutes. And Marge told me where you are going and why."

Wai Gong wandered over to us. "Are we going to Blackpool now?" he asked me.

"Yes, we're going right now," I told him. I looked at him and wondered again what was going on with Wai Gong. Was it more than just sadness? I took his hand. "I'm going to get you to Blackpool, Wai Gong, and nothing is going to stop us." I patted my jacket pocket, which was where I had put the tickets for the Tower Ballroom. They were safe at least.

Marge gave me a hug. "Lizzie, you remind me of my great-grandmother Lizzie—she was a determined lass too. I think you should keep going. Minh will get over it. It's just one day, and then you'll be home."

"But now we don't have money for the train tickets," Tyler said.

"He's right. We worked so hard having a car wash, and it was all for nothing," Chi said. "I even broke one of my nails."

"Violet, the kids can have our spare change collection," Marge said. She pointed to the corner of the counter, where a glass jar was filled with coins. It said MARGE'S ANGELS COMMUNITY FUND. "It's to help those in need, and you need it right now."

"You've already helped us by bringing us here. I can't ask for more help from you," I said.

"Nonsense. Do you believe in karma?" Dot asked. "We bikers do, even though Rhonda is pagan and thinks we should become a biker witches' coven. We all try to live life to the fullest, and we want you all to do that as well. Get your grandad on that dance floor!"

I didn't know if I believed in karma, but I was seeing first-hand how kind people could be. And if an offer of help came out of the blue, perhaps I needed to just grab it. I could take everyone to Blackpool without Minh.

"I don't think we should take that," I said, still feeling undeserving. It could go to the children's hospital.

"No, I want you to have it," Marge said. "You're doing such a wonderful thing."

"Definitely, you deserve it," added Dot.

Rhonda nodded.

"Okay, then. Thank you so much!" I said.

Violet waddled over to the corner of the counter and lifted the large glass jar. She plonked it on the table in front of Chi, Tyler, and me. "Here you go!"

Chi sidled over to me and tapped me on the arm. "Come on, we've got to go!" I could see she was mega-excited to be ditching her brother.

"Come on, Wai Gong, we're going now."

"I've had a lovely time here, Lizzie," he said. "Such lovely ladies, but I am so excited to go. Blackpool is waiting for me!"

"Just go down the hill, and the station's on the right by the garage. You can't miss it. If you get a train now, you'll probably be there just after lunchtime," Rhonda said.

We could see Minh on the phone outside; he was shaking his head and had his hand on his forehead. He was getting quite the telling off.

"Thank you so much for your help. Tell Minh that we'll be okay without him and not to follow us," I said.

"Come on, Mr. Chu, we're going to get the train, but we've got to hurry," Chi said. The sandwiches had given her a new lease on life. "Lizzie, take Minh's camera—we can record some stuff for him. Then he won't be so mad."

I did as Chi suggested and took Minh's camera from the table.

We gave the bikers hugs and said we would keep in touch, then bundled out the back door. Our bellies were full, and we had a glass jar filled with money, a mildly confused grandad, and no big brother. The journey to the west was on again!

CHAPTER TWENTY-FOUR

Back on Track

We jogged as fast as we could down the hill until we saw the rickety old garage, Wai Gong only just managing to keep up with us. A sign saying BAMBER BRIDGE TRAIN STATION pointed down some steps. We ran over to the entrance. It was a tiny station—just a platform and a small ticket booth.

"Four singles to Blackpool," I said in a hurry. I looked to see if Minh was following us.

The price appeared on the screen, and I emptied what seemed like hundreds of coins onto the counter in front of the man, who was not very impressed.

"The train is due in five minutes. There's no way I'm going to count all of that."

"Everyone! Come here and count out thirty-four pounds," I said. "We've only got a few minutes!"

The four of us started to put the coins into piles. Our fingers worked hard. By the time we could hear the train coming, we had thirty piles—just four more to make. Tyler worked fast; his nimble fingers came in handy. Wai Gong counted like a human abacus; it surprised me how fast he was doing it. For someone who had been forgetting a lot, he certainly remembered how to count money.

The train pulled up, the man behind the counter pressed a button, and four white tickets shot out of the machine. I grabbed them.

"THANK YOU!" I yelled with glee as the four of us ran to the door of the train. We were going to make it! We jumped aboard, and then the whistle sounded and we were off!

I looked out the window as the train began to chug away.

Just then, a familiar face appeared outside. It was Minh!

He looked sweaty and angry. "Come back!" he shouted. "Chi, you can't go without me! Mum and Dad are going to kill me!"

As the train chugged away, Minh got smaller and smaller. The bikers appeared behind the fence running adjacent to the tracks, beeping their horns and flashing their headlights. They had come to give us a proper send-off!

"That was brilliant!" Chi exclaimed. "Take that, Minh Pham! You can't stop Mr. Chu's journey to the west! Blackpool is on the west coast, isn't it?"

"It is," I said.

"He's really angry," Tyler said. "I wouldn't want to be in your shoes when you get home, Chi." He laughed.

"Finally! I am doing something without my big brother chaperoning me! My parents are going to be angry for, like, a day, but this is so much fun now that Minh is gone."

"I can't believe we made it!" I said. I felt elated. Things were back on track. Literally.

Tyler was looking at the camera, trying to work out the buttons. He aimed the lens in our direction. The red light on the side of the camera was on.

"Okay, I am going to do some recording now for Minh. Just talk and act natural. Maybe ask your grandad some stuff?"

"Can you tell me more about Grandma Kam when she was younger?" I asked Wai Gong.

"She loved sweets," said Wai Gong. "A lot of Chinese people don't like very sweet things, but not Kam. That's why she wanted to work in the bakery, you know. She wanted to make lovely sweet treats for people. Her favorite candy was those little Love Heart ones. You know, the ones with the words on them?" I nodded. "She gave me one when we met at the Blackpool Tower Ballroom for the first time—it said FOREVER. I ate it, but I wish I had kept it instead."

"Sweets are for eating though, that's their whole purpose," said Chi. "If you'd kept the sweet for however many years, I reckon the word would have faded and it would have gone all chalky and moldy. I think it's best that you ate it, since you made your wife happy in that moment too. And now you have the memory inside you forever."

I didn't know where the old Chi had gone, but this new one was much kinder.

"I remember Love Hearts. She used to buy those for me too when I was younger if I was crying. She'd find the one that said DON'T CRY and give it to me, which always made me laugh," I said.

"She was awesome," Tyler said. "You must miss her a lot, Lizzie."

"I do," I said quietly.

"Remember when you bought us a lobster from the Chinese supermarket for the Lunar New Year, and I was upset because it was still alive, and I wanted to set it free?" I asked Wai Gong. "But I was too scared to pick it up because it had massive claws, so I put on oven mitts, but then I dropped it and it ran into the living room?" I laughed, remembering how I'd screamed.

"I don't remember a lobster, Lizzie. Are you sure it was me who brought it home? Why can't I remember that?" Wai Gong said.

I held his hand. "It's okay, don't worry about that." I knew now that the way he'd been forgetting things maybe wasn't so normal. But I didn't want to make him more anxious about not being able to remember the lobster incident. I racked my memory for other things he might recall us doing as a family.

"Wai Gong, do you remember when I was about seven, sometimes you and Grandma Kam would do qigong together in the park while I played on the jungle gym? I hurt my knee one time because I fell off. And you sat me down and taught me how to hold the golden sun pose, and it helped me calm down and forget about my knee hurting?"

"Yes! I remember that! Kam and I loved dancing, but we also loved qigong. Dancing was our yang activity, fast and powerful. And qigong was our yin activity. It helped us to cope with becoming parents again. The slowness of the movements helped us focus on what was right in front of us, which was you, Lizzie." Wai Gong smiled at me.

I knew he was talking about my mother. It must have been so hard for them to lose their daughter, and then I was there to take care of. They'd not had much time to come to terms with it before there were diapers to change.

"That's great, Mr. Chu," Chi said.

"I want to do some now!" Wai Gong said, leaping up out of his seat.

Here? Right now? On the train?

I was going to stop him, but as I rose, Chi put her hand gently on my arm.

"Let him do it, Lizzie, it might help," she said.

I sat back down in my seat.

Wai Gong took a deep breath in. He proceeded to hold an imaginary beach ball between his palms. The other passengers in the train car looked on with concern as my grandad blew air out of his lips while moving his arms in a churning motion.

He walked into the main aisle, and a couple of very large, buff, rugby-type guys began laughing at him. I had an uneasy feeling in my stomach. I hoped it wasn't going to escalate. I'd heard about people being racist to people of color on public transport, where there wasn't anywhere to run. I leaned over the side of my chair to check out who else we were sharing a car with. Farther down was a group wearing fleece tops that said MUSLIM RAMBLERS ASSOCIATION. They had those metal walking sticks leaning against the side of the luggage rack.

"Come, everyone stand up and do some stretching and qigong with me! You don't have to sit there being bored; we can move together!" Wai Gong told everyone in the car.

The biggest rugby guy nodded and stood up near his seat. "Me shoulders are tight, actually," he said with a thick York-shire accent. He started rotating his big beefy arms in the air like Wai Gong.

Then a woman with a sleeping baby in a car seat also stood up and began copying Wai Gong. The other rugby guy raised his eyebrows and shrugged, then got up too. Chi's dad would have been well impressed, being a yoga teacher and all.

"Is this how you do it?" the mum asked. "I've been getting sore wrists from breastfeeding. The angle must be wrong." Wai Gong nodded at the woman, encouraging her to move her body. He had his hands on his hips now and began swiveling them around and around. The Muslim walkers also stood up and started to rotate their shoulders.

"This is just what I need after that walk, thanks," one said.

"I've got to limber up for the dancing. You know, great dancers do a lot of stretching before a performance," Wai Gong said.

A grey-haired man in a uniform came rushing down the aisle. I thought he was going tell off Wai Gong and order everyone to sit in their seats. Instead, he put down his ticket machine and started shaking his hips too and giving everyone high fives.

I felt like I was living in a dreamland. It was wonderful to see Wai Gong coming to life like this.

Tyler smiled at me and whispered, "He's having fun, Lizzie; you can relax a little."

I nodded.

"Come, Guan Yin, you too. Get up and move your body," Wai Gong said. He held his hand out to Chi, who was reluctant at first, then got up and moved her arms around very slowly in tai chi waves.

"Waving hands to the east, waving hands to the west," she said. She whispered to me, "My dad taught me that in family yoga. It's more of a tai chi thing, but everything is a fusion these days, isn't it?"

Wai Gong stretched up and then sat down. The passengers who had taken part in the impromptu stretching and qigong session gave him a round of applause. One of the Muslim Ramblers leaned over and pressed a ten-pound note into Wai Gong's hand.

"This is for you, sir," he said.

"Final station, Blackpool!" said the conductor as he walked off down the aisle. Everyone began putting on their coats and picking up their bags.

I smiled as we entered the station. I grabbed Wai Gong's hand. "We made it, we're here. We're going to be okay," I told him, and gave his hand a little squeeze.

The Arrival

"Where to now, oh Divine One?" Wai Gong said as we left the station in Blackpool.

"Follow me, Mr. Chu, we're going to the magical sea!" Chi said, waving her arms. Tyler laughed.

"She's really improving. I give her performance a three out of ten," he said.

Chi flicked his forehead in annoyance. "Look, if you think you can do a better job of being a fake goddess, be my guest!" Chi said. She was smiling, so I knew she was feeling all right.

"Okay, we've got three hours before tea. Why don't we go to the Pleasure Beach amusements first and you can go on some rides? I don't want you to come all this way and not have fun too," I said.

"But we don't have enough money for tickets for the rides," Tyler said.

"You're right, we've only got ten pounds," Chi said. She pouted. "I really wanted to go on the Waltzer!"

"Me too!" said Wai Gong, "What is it?" he added, clueless.

"They're like giant magical buckets that twirl you around and around!" Chi said. "They make you feel like throwing up, but they're awesome!"

"Let's head that way and we can figure it out. Maybe there will be a miracle," I said.

We walked in pairs toward the promenade. The sea air smelled of freshly deep-fried doughnuts, and a cool breeze made the sides of my hair flutter.

The majestic red metallic frame of Blackpool Tower was in the distance. The Mecca of ballroom dancing was in our sights. I was closer to accomplishing our mission. Wai Gong had a spring in his step. He seemed taller and breathed in the air deeply.

"Ahhh, Lizzie, it feels so good to be out of the city. Kam is here. I can feel her in the wind, the way it brushes against my face. Can you feel her too?"

I looked around. It was nice, but we were still not quite at the beach yet, and we were walking past a set of overflowing recycling bins. So no, I couldn't really feel her here. But I didn't want to burst his bubble.

"Yes, I can feel her here with us," I said.

"Goddess, thank you so much for bringing us to Blackpool," Wai Gong said to Chi. "It means so much to me. This journey with you all is very special. We really are on a pilgrimage together, just like Monkey, Tripitaka, Sandy, and Pigsy. It's just like that." Wai Gong was practically skipping along the pavement.

Chi began to giggle, then stopped moving and patted her side. She pulled out her phone, which was vibrating. Her face was taut.

"Uh-oh," she said. "Mum's calling, and I've got a gazillion missed calls from Minh, who is no doubt very annoyed with me, but he'll get over it."

"Are you going to answer it?" I asked, knowing that Jane was going to give Chi an earful.

She looked reluctant. "I suppose I'd better . . ." she said, and she walked off to the side, tapping the green button. I could tell from her expression that things were not great. Her face was contorted into a grimace when she returned to us.

"Everything all right?" Tyler asked.

"Mum's fuming, as you would expect. She's had to pay someone to work in the café last-minute. She and Dad are going to pick up Minh first, then drive here. They'll meet us at the Tower later," Chi said.

"We'd better go have some fun before they arrive," Tyler said.

"Yeah! Let's have some fun before the oldies arrive and ruin it all!" Chi began to run along the promenade, arms out so her sleeves flapped behind her like swan wings. She caught up to Wai Gong and put her hand up for a high five. He didn't know what to do at first, because usually he bowed and prayed to the goddess, but then he got into the spirit and gave her a high five back.

We walked farther along and found some steps down to the beach. It wasn't exactly like those sandy beaches you saw in TV commercials for vacations with sun loungers and blue water. It was sort of brown and damp. There weren't that many people on the beach. A man with his cockapoo off the leash, a boy trying to get his kite to fly, and one person in a wet suit who was going to brave the cold, choppy water.

I took the camera from Tyler and started to film panoramic shots of the beach. I knew this was the first time Tyler had ever been to the seaside. It didn't exactly look like a beach in California or the Costa del Sol, but we didn't care. We were here. We'd made it.

"Ta-da! Ty, we're here. We're at the seaside, and there is the ocean. How do you feel?" I asked, pointing the lens at his face. He looked excited and a little in awe.

"Whoa! It's odd. It's like . . . so weird that there is nothing there in front of me, no buildings, no trees. It's awesome, Lizzie. Thanks for letting me tag along." Tyler grinned wide as he took in the sea before him. He opened his arms and breathed in the salty air, which also smelled of greasy food and vinegar. He took a selfie with the sea behind him and texted it to his dads. We heard his phone ping, and Tyler laughed.

"They told me to have fun!" He smiled.

We all walked closer to the edge of the water.

"Go on, then, go paddling in the sea!" Chi said.

I got the camera in position to film Tyler's first time in the sea. He took off his shoes and socks and walked into the brownish water that was coming up to greet him.

"Ahhhhh! It's so cold!" he said, his knees knocking together. He quickly retreated to where his shoes lay on the shore. I handed him the camera and took off my sneakers and socks.

"My turn," I said. The sand squished between my toes like brown sludge. Wai Gong took his shoes and socks off too, exposing his toes. The big toe on his right foot was slightly black from when he'd dropped a brick on it by accident.

We sat on the beach for a while in silence, just staring out at the horizon. The wind was strong, whipping our hair and Chi's robe into a frenzy. The sea was hypnotizing. Seagulls glided overhead.

Wai Gong stood up and faced the water. He looked like he was in a trance, and he even looked younger somehow.

"How do you like the beach?" I asked. "Do you remember it being like this?"

"It's amazing, Lizzie," he said. "I can feel my soul expanding . . . it's getting bigger and bigger." He stretched out his arms like he was going to hug the sea.

"We'd better get down to Pleasure Beach if we're going to go on any rides," Chi said. "It's one thirty already."

"Let me just get some more shots for Minh, hang on," Tyler said. He got out Minh's camera and started filming us on the beach. Then he filmed the sea and panned around to take in the promenade, the Tower in the distance, the piers, and the blue sky.

Chi and Wai Gong began walking arm in arm, talking about something. Chi was even laughing. Tyler and I followed behind them.

"You okay?" he asked me.

I nodded. "Yeah, I'm good. I'm just thinking about family stuff. This trip has brought up a lot of . . . questions and things. I guess I've never been part of a 'normal' family, have I?"

"What's normal? People think the same about me. Having two dads *is* my normal. It might not be what everyone understands, but it's my reality, and this is yours. Try being a Black boy with two dads. It's not always the easiest, you know."

"I know . . . and thanks, Ty. I feel better talking about it all. Like I'm not so alone. There were days when I didn't think this trip was going to happen. It's been hard sometimes, *really* hard."

"I know, Lizzie, but look what you did. You got him to Blackpool. You got us all here—you didn't give up."

"Yeah, I did that. Let's make this day count, then," I said.

Tyler nodded and put his arm around me. "You're the best granddaughter he could ever have wished for, Lizzie."

Tyler and I linked arms, and we followed the goddess and my grandad down the beach to the theme park.

CHAPTER TWENTY-SIX

Blackpool Pleasure Beach

The wind blew Chi's flowing costume all over the place as she walked along the damp sand. Her hairpieces were lopsided, and I couldn't help but laugh as I observed her from behind. Tyler and I caught up to her and Wai Gong.

"You look like a goddess who's been spun around inside a washing machine," I said.

"I'm freezing. I wish I'd put on leggings under this robe," she said. "You didn't tell me it was going to be so cold!"

We'd strolled past South Pier already, and the Pleasure Beach rides were in front of us. I was sad that we didn't have enough money to buy wristbands for rides. I knew Tyler felt really bad about it.

"Mr. Chu, are you enjoying Blackpool so far?" said Tyler. We walked up the steps to the main promenade. Stalls lined the sides of the street and gaggles of tourists moved up and down.

"It's wonderful. The sea. The fresh air. I like it very much," said Wai Gong. He was looking around excitedly at the colorful displays. The smell of cotton candy wafted into my nostrils. But we had to be careful with our money—we had only the ten pounds Wai Gong had earned on the train from his qigong performance and a few pennies left over from the jar.

Wai Gong was smiling. He headed toward a kiosk that had hats that said KISS ME QUICK, and I pulled a face. *Yuck!* I hoped he didn't want one of those. What little money we did have was for food. He started pulling out sticks of rock candy one at a time and putting them on the kiosk in front of the server.

"We don't have enough money for those," I told him.

"Are you going to buy those, mate?" the man asked Wai Gong.

"No, no, we're all right, thanks," I said. But it was too late. Wai Gong had ripped off the cellophane and was sucking on a black-and-white striped stick of candy. Then he pulled a face and put it down on the counter.

"Ergh, too sweet, too sweet," he said, smiling at the man who was holding out his hand.

"That will be three pounds, thank you very much."

I begrudgingly handed over the ten-pound note and then pocketed the change.

"There's no way we can all go on a ride with only seven pounds between us," I told Tyler and Chi. "I'm so sorry. I really wanted you to have a good time at Pleasure Beach."

"Ah! I've just remembered! I can pay for everyone!" said Wai Gong jubilantly. He took out a wad of twenty-pound notes rolled up in an elastic band from inside his pocket. Tyler, Chi, and I all stood with our mouths open. Flies could have landed inside and set up camp on our tongues.

"He hasn't ripped off Violet's café, has he?" asked Chi.

"There's no way, Chi! Don't even say something like that!" I blurted out.

"It's a lot of money, Lizzie," Tyler said.

"No, he wouldn't do something like that!" I turned to Wai Gong. "Where did you get all that money from?"

"The goddess has provided and will continue to bless us. We don't have to worry, Lizzie. We will be cared for, just you wait and see. You worry too much!"

Wai Gong ran over to the building where you buy wristbands before I could stop him. He gave the bored-looking woman on the other side of the glass money for four wristbands. She passed them through the window before I could object.

"I don't know what to do with him. I think that must be our money for rent and bills," I said, wondering how we were ever going to replace it.

"Lizzie, let's just have fun, okay? The goddess here, which is me, says we can sort it all out later," Chi said.

"It's all right for you two. You've never had the electricity shut off or had a fridge without food in it. You don't know what it's been like for me, having to deal with those things."

"You're twelve, Lizzie," Tyler said. "Chi's right, it's okay to be twelve and have fun. You deserve it, not just your grandad. This trip is for you too."

Wai Gong came back over to us and held out four purple wristbands. Tyler took one and wrapped it around my wrist.

"Tell yourself you can have fun," he said.

I smiled at him. Then I put a wristband on him.

Chi put on hers. "Thanks, Mr. Chu," she said.

We walked through the entrance under the Noah's Ark and headed into the security area. A guard quickly looked in our bags and ushered us through the turnstiles into the amusement park.

Wai Gong and Chi looked at each other and grinned, then ran over to the roller coaster. There was a queue, but it wasn't too bad. Tyler and I followed. Soon it was our turn to board the ride.

"Come sit with me, Lizzie," Wai Gong said. I nodded and smiled. Tyler and Chi were right. I should enjoy this day instead of always trying to control things or being afraid it would all come tumbling down.

We got into the seats. Wai Gong pulled down his harness, the blue tubes holding him in tight. I did the same. I felt nervous, butterflies swirling around in my belly. The roller coaster began to move forward, the chains *click-clack*ing as we gathered speed. And then we dropped suddenly!

"WOO-HOO!" shouted Chi. "I love Blackpool!"

The roller coaster sped up as it followed the orange track, throwing the car side to side. Wai Gong was giggling. I put my hand over my mouth—what if I got sick on us both? That would be the worst.

"Aaaaaaaaaaaarrrrrrgggggghhhhhhhhhhhh!" I let out the biggest scream I could. And it felt good to let it all out. "Woooooooo! Yes!"

I felt free for the first time in ages. The wind blasted through my hair; my fingers were holding on for dear life. My belly flip-flopped all over the place. Then we turned into a corkscrew and went upside down! *Whoosh!*

"Yes!" Wai Gong shouted, clapping his hands. "Yes! Godddessss!"

Chi screamed out behind me, "This is heaven!" Even Tyler was laughing as we circled back to the beginning. Our seats jolted into place. The ride had ended.

The mechanism clicked, and we lifted our harnesses up and woozily stepped out of the car. My knees felt wobbly.

"Wai Gong, are you okay?" I asked. He was bent over with his hands on his knees, and his shoulders were going up and down. I thought he was having trouble breathing.

"Am I okay? That was the best time, Lizzie." He was bent over laughing. Tears streamed down his face. "I never will forget this day." He turned to Chi and Tyler, who were getting out of their car.

Chi patted my back. "Well done not throwing up!" Her face was flushed, her cheeks rosy.

Tyler had a quick look at the camera, which had been on the whole time. "I got some cool shots for Minh," he said.

"That was awesome," I said. "Thanks for encouraging me to go."

Chi nodded. "Perhaps I'm not a goddess only for your gramps. You need a little magic in your life too, Lizzie."

Wai Gong was grinning. "Thank you, Kam, for providing the money for these rides!" He looked up and put his palms together, lifting them to the sky.

"What? How did Grandma Kam pay for the rides?" I had a bad feeling I wasn't going to like what he was about to tell me.

"I took the gold necklace with the jade on it and went to one of those pawn shops and swapped it for cash."

"No! What? You really did that? That was my gift from her, Wai Gong!" I put my hands on my forehead. If they'd sold it to someone, I'd never be able to get it back. Even though I was usually the cynical one, I'd felt like that necklace was lucky. Maybe his swapping it for cash had been the reason things had been going wrong since we'd left home?

"Did I do something wrong?" Wai Gong said.

Tyler gently shook his head.

"Take a deep breath, Lizzie, and breathe out through kissy lips," said Chi. "Slowly, like you're blowing a dandelion—

my dad taught us that in family yoga. It helps when I'm really stressed about something."

I did as Chi said. It took a while to not feel like my head was going to implode, but I eventually calmed down.

"Family yoga isn't all that bad, then, is it?" I said, smiling.

We had so much fun at Pleasure Beach. Wai Gong was interested in the arcades and played three rounds of a game where you roll balls up a ramp so your camel moves forward. He didn't win but was happy to see them racing one another. He gave us all some money to spend on the arcade machines. Chi and I raced against each other in matching cars. Tyler managed to win a teddy bear the size of a small child, which he gave to a boy in a wheelchair who was passing with his dad.

I noticed that the sun was low in the sky and the light was starting to fade.

"What time is it?" I asked Tyler.

"It's four forty-five," he told me.

"Come on, we need to run!" I shouted.

We legged it down the promenade as the light faded. It was at least a thirty-minute walk down to the Tower Ballroom. The Tower loomed in the darkening skyline in the distance. I'd had no idea that Blackpool was so big. I was starting to worry as we rushed past fish and chip shops and pubs.

"I can't run anymore!" moaned Chi, flopping down on a metal bus shelter bench. We stopped.

"You can't stop now! We've got to carry on!" I demanded. Chi scowled and began rubbing her feet.

"You carry on, I'll stay here," Chi said.

"If she is staying, then I am staying," Wai Gong said, sitting down next to her. This was not what I needed right now.

An old lady with a flowery jacket sat next to Chi. "Tram should be here in a second. I made it just in time!"

"We can't give up! We've been through so much to get here," I said.

"The goddess will give us a sign, Lizzie. Just have faith," Wai Gong said. His calmness was both reassuring and infuriating.

Just then, the Blackpool Illuminations that flanked both sides of the road along the Golden Mile lit up. They went on for what felt like miles.

"Look!" said Chi. "The lights all came on just when he said that. Did you see that?"

They were colorful and arranged in different shapes and patterns. The ones nearest us were in the shape of crystal balls, each with a different object inside. Was it a sign?

CHAPTER TWENTY-SEVEN

To the Tower!

Somehow Wai Gong was right, because just then a purple tram pulled up beside us and opened its doors. We weren't sitting at a bus stop—we were at the tram stop! I should have noticed all the wires overhead. Luckily for us, it was headed in the direction we needed to go. We let the lady in the flowery jacket get on first.

"See, I knew we would get divine help. We will make it, Lizzie!" Wai Gong said. He put a twenty-pound note in front of the driver. "To the Mecca of ballroom!" he said, swaying down the aisle with his hands on his hips.

"Don't you want your change?" asked the driver, counting how many of us there were.

"Yes, thanks!" I said as I grabbed the coins. Chi and Tyler followed and sat down on the comfy seats.

"Ahhhh, it feels so good to sit down!" Chi said. She grimaced when she looked at the bottom of her robe and her now-stained sneakers. She was the dirtiest goddess I had ever seen.

"How long till we get to the Tower?" I asked the lady from the tram stop.

"Around twelve minutes. Are you in a rush?" she asked.

"We're going there for afternoon tea, but we're late."

"Oh, it's lovely, dear. Make sure you try the Victoria sponge cake—it's so soft. I'll let you know when to get off."

My leg started to jiggle nervously. The lady patted my hand. "Don't worry, dear, it'll be all right. I've got a sixth sense," she said.

I wanted to hug this stranger next to me. Perhaps it would be all right in the end. Only another few minutes to go. *Calm down, Lizzie, we're nearly there.* I did the slow breathing thing Chi had told me about. Tyler was adjusting her headpiece and trying to pin some of the material to the front of her costume with safety pins to hide some of the stains.

I looked at my friends and my grandad. I was lucky to have them here. We were so close now. My stomach gurgled, and the lady next to me heard it.

"Here, have this." She pushed a digestive biscuit into my hand, then gave Tyler, Chi, and Wai Gong one each. "If I don't share them out, I'll eat them all. Got to watch my figure." She grinned.

"Thanks so much," I said. I was starving. Wai Gong and the others started to eat theirs. The universe really was providing for us now.

"Get off at the next stop," said the lady. She pushed the red button on the rail for us. "Enjoy every moment." She winked at me. She reminded me of my grandma: warm, cuddly, always giving me sweet treats.

We stood up, and I waved at her as we got off. The entrance to the Tower was across the street. We ran over.

"Ohhh, we're really here!" shouted Wai Gong.

"We are, Mr. Chu," said Chi. She smiled at me. "Come on, let's go!"

"Wait, before we go in, I've got something for you . . . a surprise," Tyler said. He knelt down, opened the massive rucksack he had been lugging around the whole day, and took out a plastic bag.

"For me?" i asked. i had wondered why Tyler had bought such a big bag with him. Now I knew.

"Lizzie, this is for you." He pulled out a black tuxedo with satin lapels, a bow tie, and a white shirt. Tyler had made me my very own fancy suit just like the ones on TV, but this one was even better!

"I thought you deserved your own fancy outfit too. My dad helped me to make it."

"Oh my god, Ty! I love it so much! You know me so well." I gave him the biggest hug. "Where can I change though? We're already late."

"We'll stand with our backs to you and act as a shield," Chi said, holding up her robe to block out any prying eyes. I quickly wriggled into my new outfit, fit for a ballroom. I still had my old scruffy Converse on, but I didn't care. I handed Tyler my other clothes, which he tucked into his bag. I hugged him again so hard I thought I might squeeze him to death.

"Tyler, your dads should be so proud of you for being able to make something like this," I said. "It fits perfectly."

We needed to go now. Time was running out.

The red brick was clean and the pillars outside impressive. We all looked up at the top of the Tower. I had to make sure we found the right room, because there were loads of attractions at the Blackpool Tower: a circus, a dungeon, the actual tower, and much more.

The four of us looked very strange: me in my fabulous tux; Tyler in his blue jacket and jeans; Wai Gong in his suit and tie from the eighties. Chi was getting stared at in her stained and rumpled Guan Yin outfit.

The lobby was huge and had a miniature model of the Tower in a glass case. I saw a sign that read TOWER BALL-ROOM to the right—level two.

"Up the stairs, everyone!" I yelled.

CHAPTER TWENTY-EIGHT

Too Late

We ran up the stairs. Wai Gong stopped to admire the turquoise-blue ceramic tiles that were embedded in the red brick as we went. "Look, Lizzie, there's a fish flying here in the tiles."

"We can't dawdle!" I told the others. I never used the word *dawdle*; it was one of Grandma Kam's words. I urged everyone to carry on to level two.

"We're here!" I said in jubilation. We had reached the frosted doors, which read WELCOME TO THE BLACKPOOL TOWER BALLROOM. I opened the door, and inside was another door. I stopped to catch my breath.

A man wearing a black uniform with gold trim sat in a chair behind a small wooden desk. I ran over and placed the four tickets on the desk. The man picked them up and looked at them closely. He frowned, then looked straight at me, not saying anything for a moment.

"I'm sorry, but these tickets were for yesterday, the eighteenth. Today is the nineteenth of November." The man's pale skin looked blotchy as he moved his eyes to something on the screen before him.

"What? That can't be right!" I racked my brain. "Wai Gong, you said these were for *Sunday* the eighteenth when we opened the tickets." How could this be happening?

"Did I say something wrong?" Wai Gong said.

The man held out the tickets to show me. I took them and got out my phone to check the date against them. He was right. The tickets were for Saturday, November eighteenth, which was yesterday.

I wanted to kick myself. How had I gotten it so wrong? I should have double-checked everything, but there had been so much going on!

Chi stepped forward, and a big smile spread across her face. "Please, isn't there anything you can do for us? We've come a long way for this. Those two people there"— she pointed at Wai Gong and me—"it's for them that we're here. Her grandma left them the tickets on her deathbed. Please?" Chi begged.

"Honestly, there's nothing I can do now that the date has passed. I can't even give you a refund or anything."

"No way, mister!" Chi pushed back her robe sleeves; her face was getting red. Her goddess demeanor had faded away now. I put my hand on her arm and shook my head.

"Oh jeez," said Tyler. He took the tickets to have a look himself. "I guess that's it, then."

"We've come all the way from Scotland. Our car broke down, and we had to hitch rides. Please, you have to let us in!" I was truly desperate for this man to show us the kindness that others had shown us today. There was no way this was the end. Our special journey could not end *outside* the door of the Tower Ballroom, the Mecca of ballroom where my grandparents had met.

"What's the matter, Lizzie? Why aren't we going in?" Wai Gong asked me.

I crumpled to the floor and put my head on my knees.

"Did I do something wrong?" Wai Gong asked.

"No, Mr. Chu, it's going to be all right," said Tyler. "There's been a mix-up, but I'm sure we can sort it out."

"It's over, Ty. Just leave it," I said.

We'd come so far.

Chi pulled me up and walked us away from the wooden doors that stood between us and the Tower Ballroom dance floor. My knees felt like they were about to buckle. All that effort for nothing.

Chi put her arm around me. "I'm so sorry, Lizzie."

"I'm sorry, Chi. You got dressed up for nothing," I told her.

"Are you kidding me? I've had the best time. Who knew that being a goddess for a day would be so much fun?"

"You know, Monkey, Tripitaka, Sandy, and Pigsy didn't give up," said Wai Gong. "We don't have to either!"

"He's right," said Tyler. "Guan Yin would have come down on her cloud or whatever she floats upon, and she would have helped them find another way. There must be a way we can sneak in there."

"That's true, I would have," said Chi, nodding in agreement. "As a goddess, I can honestly say that giving up isn't in my vocabulary. But we kinda need a miracle right about now."

"Where are we going to get one of those, Goddess?" I said. I just didn't know how we could get inside now.

I looked at my best friends. They weren't giving up, and neither was I. I nodded. But then I noticed Wai Gong had wandered off.

"Wai Gong! Come back!" I called. He had found another model Blackpool Tower in a glass case. But as Chi and I approached him, a man in a tuxedo ran up to Wai Gong.

"There you are! Come on, we need you in the back so you can get changed! The birthday cake is going out in fifteen minutes!"

Wai Gong looked as confused as Chi, Tyler, and I felt.

"Erm, hello . . . can I ask what you are talking about?" I asked.

The man craned his neck to look at Wai Gong's face. "You're the Chinese Elvis, aren't you? You got here okay! Someone told me you might be late, as there was a lot of traffic, but you're right on time! Follow me!"

"Who's Elvis, and was he Chinese?" I asked Chi and Tyler.

"Duh, Elvis Presley is that famous old singer," Chi said.

"They called him the King of Rock 'n' Roll, and there are loads of singers who impersonate him. There must be one who is Chinese, even though Elvis wasn't Chinese himself," Tyler said.

"We've got to hurry," said the man. "Who are you three? I didn't know there was going to be an entourage too."

"I'm his stylist, and she's his manager," said Chi, pointing to me.

The man looked confused.

"And I'm the cameraman," added Tyler. "We're hoping to get footage for a new show reel, if that's okay?" Tyler got out the camera and showed it to the man.

"Fine, fine, but we must get a move on."

He led us around the side to a different entrance from the one ticket holders used. We followed him to a set of dressing rooms. He opened the door and sat Wai Gong down in front of a mirror with lightbulbs all around its edges.

"Your costume arrived earlier by courier. It's hung up over there, and your wig is on the glass head on the table. There are complimentary pastries, and the table you're going to serenade is number thirty-two. You're up in ten minutes! You got that, old-timer?" he asked, looking at Wai Gong. "The lady is sixty today, and you're to sing the song 'Burning Love.' Is that okay?

You can do another one if you want. Then we've got the regular tea dance happening. You three: Keep to the sides when he's working, okay? You can go up to the balcony to film if you want," he said, pointing to Tyler. "There's a spare table you can sit at if you want to stay afterward. It has a card that says 'Reserved for Elvis.' There will be complimentary food for you too."

"Sure thing, mister, sounds amazing," said Chi, practically pushing him out the door. "We'll be fine. He's a professional . . . the best in the world."

"Ten minutes, and remember it's table thirty-two!" The man zoomed out the door.

"Mr. Chu, that kind gentleman has left this Elvis outfit for you," Chi said, holding up the white sequined jumpsuit with flared legs.

Wai Gong grabbed it from Chi. "I LOVE IT!" he said. "Lizzie, this is the best day ever! I've always loved the King of Rock 'n' Roll!" He went behind a curtain and put on the outfit. It was a little tight around the waist, and Tyler couldn't zip it to the top, so he safety-pinned it.

"You look . . . fantastic!" I told him, chuckling. The Tower Ballroom dance floor was just a few meters away. We'd get to dance together after all!

"Right, Mr. Chu! It's showtime!" Chi said. "To end our fabulous journey to the west, your final mission is to sing to a woman who is sixty years old at table number thirty-two. Is that okay?"

"This is so exciting. I love to sing!"

I patted him on the back. Tyler got out the camera and filmed Wai Gong, who was getting into character by wobbling his lip and shaking his hips around.

"This outfit is even better to dance in!" Wai Gong said.

I began to laugh. Who would have thought Wai Gong would be mistaken for an Elvis impersonator?

"Mr. Chu, sit down, please, so I can get this Elvis hair on properly." Chi picked up the gelled wig and pulled it over Wai Gong's head. It slid over his eyes a little. The Chinese Elvis who had been booked had a much bigger head than my grandfather. Every time he moved, the wig flopped over his eyes.

"I can't see," he said.

Chi looked around for something to stick the wig to Wai Gong's head, but she couldn't find anything.

"Wait! Violet not only has the best sausages in the world, she also has bees. She told me about them, and she gave me some honey!" Wai Gong said. He walked over to his suit jacket, took a small jar filled with golden stuff from its pocket, and opened it. He smeared a little on his fingers and then smoothed it along his hairline. It was a day for miracles, because the honey worked! The Elvis wig was now well and truly stuck to his head.

"Okay, yeah, that's definitely *not* gross, Mr. Chu!" Chi said, squirming.

We all headed for the door. This was it. I was going to see the Tower Ballroom in person for the very first time. My belly was flip-flopping. Chi took my arm and held Wai Gong's on the other side.

"Let's go!" Wai Gong said. "To the Tower Ballroom!"

We skipped down the corridor toward a large set of doors.

CHAPTER TWENTY-NINE

Cha-Cha

When we entered the ballroom, I held my breath for a moment or two. It was just so grand. The stage was flanked by thick red velvet curtains with a lamppost at either side. At the back was the bar and the food area with glass cases full of cakes. The ceiling was covered in decorations. It was even more magnificent in real life. I held back a tear as we walked along the red patterned carpet and past the marble pillars to the main area. We'd made it.

"I'm going to go upstairs and film some footage," said Tyler. He took Minh's camera and went to a side door, then reappeared in the corner of the first balcony. I gave him a little wave; he gave me a thumbs-up.

I watched Wai Gong as he took off his sunglasses and stared at the scene before him. The lights shone on the wooden dance floor, and around the edges, round tables covered with blue tablecloths were full of people ready to have their after-noon tea. Serving staff brought out platters of cakes and elegant triangular sandwiches with the crusts cut off, delicate pastries, and scones with clotted cream and jam.

An older couple got up from their table and started to waltz around the room to the music of the organ played by a man with his back to us. They looked like they were deeply in love. I wished Grandma Kam could have been here to see this.

"I'm in Blackpool!" Wai Gong shouted. A few people tutted and sipped their tea. "Thank you, Goddess . . . this is the best day. The best." He put his arm out toward Chi, inviting her to dance.

"Nope, I don't dance, Mr. Chu. It wasn't in my contract for me to dance, just to dress up and get you here. We should probably get you singing that Elvis song first, and then you can dance with Lizzie," Chi said.

Table number thirty-two wasn't hard to spot. Most of the women had on matching pink two-piece suits, apart from one lady, who must be Wendy, I thought. Purple and gold balloons floated above the middle of the table. A sign read HAPPY 60TH BIRTHDAY, WENDY!

"Wai Gong, are you okay?" I asked.

"Yes, Lizzie, but what am I supposed to do again?" he asked. He looked around the room. Some people were staring at him in amusement. We must have been quite the sight.

"Hey, Mr. Chu, see that lady over there with the balloons on her table? It's her sixtieth birthday today, and you just need to sing a song for her. You can do it!" Chi said.

Wai Gong went over and tapped a woman on the shoulder. She had on a blue dress with lots of fringe all over it.

"Oh my god! It's Elvis!" She wore a huge badge the size of a dinner plate that said I'M 60!

Wai Gong got down on one knee and began to sing "My Heart Will Go On" from *Titanic*; it was most definitely *not* an Elvis song, but the woman didn't care at all. Her friends clapped, and a server brought out a large birthday cake with pink icing and a photo of Elvis stuck in the middle. Wai Gong was lapping up the attention. His smile beamed as he twirled the woman around. To end the performance, he bowed and kissed the back of her hand. The woman's face flushed red. Then she began to cut her birthday cake.

I looked up and saw Tyler still filming. He looked out from behind the camera and gave a big thumbs-up with a grin.

Chi and I found the table the man had said was reserved for us and sat down. A server came over and put a cake stand with sandwiches, scones, and cakes on it, plus a pot of tea and a jug of lemonade. It was like a mini birthday party and completely made up for Wai Gong forgetting my actual birthday!

"Did you see me? I was Elvis Presley, King of Rock 'n' Roll!" Wai Gong said as he came over to join us. I stood up to give him a hug.

"We did see you! You were fantastic!" I said.

"You were awesome, Mr. Chu! And now we can eat! I'm so hungry! I feel like I haven't eaten for days," Chi said, reaching for a scone. She slathered dollops of clotted cream and strawberry jam on it and shoved it into her mouth. Her lipstick from the morning had disappeared a long time ago. She looked like a hungry banshee rather than a serene goddess.

The lights dimmed. I was confused. I thought afternoon tea at the Tower Ballroom was mainly oldies eating and drinking tea and then dancing around the floor in a circle. But different-colored lights began to swirl around the room. An emcee appeared on the dance floor.

Just then, the doors opened and a couple entered. They looked a lot younger and more glamorous than the rest of the people in the room. He was wearing a tuxedo, and he looked familiar. The woman was in a tight silver sequined off-the-shoulder dress. I looked up at Wai Gong, who held his breath as they walked past us to the dance floor.

"It's them, Lizzie!" Wai Gong uttered in total shock.

"No, it can't be—can it?"

They smiled their pearly white smiles at me. It was Milo du Peck and Carmen Piernas from *Strictly*! What were they doing here?

"It's a dream, Lizzie. The stars of *Strictly* are here?" He hugged me. Then he hugged Chi. "Thank you, Goddess!"

"No problem, always happy to help you earthlings," Chi said.

The emcee tapped the microphone. "Ladies and gentlemen, tonight we have very special guests. Milo and Carmen from *Strictly Come Dancing* are taking time out from their busy schedule to surprise Milo's auntie Wendy, whose sixtieth birthday is today! They will perform the cha-cha. Please do join in when the lights go up, if you know the steps!"

I couldn't believe it. Wai Gong had serenaded Milo du Peck's auntie! The organ music stopped, and a Cuban song began playing over the sound system.

I looked at Wai Gong, aka Elvis. And he had the biggest smile on his face.

"It's really them, isn't it?" he asked me.

"It is!" I exclaimed.

This was *definitely* a sign from the universe.

The cha-cha had been Wai Gong and Grandma Kam's first dance together. Our favorite dancers were here too. I felt like I was going to explode!

"We've got to go over and dance with them!" said Wai Gong.

I felt my knees tremble slightly—I couldn't dance on the same floor as Milo du Peck and Carmen Piernas!

I looked up to Tyler and mouthed, "Come down here! I need your help!"

CHAPTER THIRTY

Two Left Cold Feet

Tyler came down from the balcony.

"What's wrong? You look like you might vomit," he said.

I did feel like bringing up my sandwich. My stomach was flipping over and over.

"I can't go out there on the dance floor. I'm going to be awful!" I said. "I can't dance in front of Milo du Peck and Carmen Piernas!"

Wai Gong had leaped up and was swaying around the dance floor, hips going from side to side.

Chi came over, took my hand, and looked at me. Her gaze was serious. "You can do it, Lizzie. Look how far we've come. You got us here despite having no money, despite our ride breaking down, despite the tickets being for the wrong day. You overcame all of that, Lizzie, and you can do this!"

I rushed to the side of the ballroom and out to the dressing room. Chi and Tyler followed me in.

"I'm not cool like you, Chi. That's why I didn't dress up at Comic Con. You can literally make a sheet look good. I'm not like that. And who am I kidding about being able to dance after learning from YouTube?"

"You learned just from watching videos on YouTube?" Chi asked.

"Yep," I replied. "I'm going to be terrible, aren't I?" My knees started to shake even more.

Tyler grabbed my shoulders and turned me around. In front of me was a long mirror.

"Look at yourself. You are the Lizster! You are rockin' that tux," Tyler said. I could hear an echo of his American dad, who said stuff like that.

I looked at myself. I did look pretty good. I'd been too distracted with getting Wai Gong ready to check out how I looked in the suit earlier. I looked fab in these trousers. And my hair was wavy. I liked how I looked.

Take that, Kiera McAllister.

"You look amazing in your tux, Lizzie. Have some confidence," Tyler said. "You always hide it away. Chi has her own thing, and you have yours. You don't need to be the best dancer at all. It's about having fun. Stop thinking and start doing! *Fake it till you make it*, remember?"

We left the dressing room and walked back to the pizzazz of the ballroom.

Wai Gong came over and held out his hand to me. "Will you dance, Lizzie?" he asked. "I need someone to dance with."

I gulped and shook my head.

Behind him, Carmen shimmied her way over and took Wai Gong's hand. "I'll dance with you, Elvis!"

A new song began, and the middle of the floor cleared. Wai Gong and Carmen started to dance, and everyone began to clap. I was in awe of the way her body and the music were so in sync. She was perfect.

And Wai Gong was brilliant! Even better than I expected. He looked twenty again. Chi, Tyler, and I watched in amazement. The couples who had been dancing stopped to watch and clap to the beat.

Wai Gong was a star.

I felt a tap on my shoulder. When I turned, Milo du Peck was standing there smiling at me. His black hair was gelled into a quiff. His dazzling smile was as white as sugar cubes.

"I've been informed by that young man in blue holding the camera that the wonderful Elvis is your grandfather. He seems to have borrowed my partner. Would you mind being my partner for this dance? Don't worry, I can lead. You just mirror me!"

Chi gave me a shove.

"Me? You want to dance with me? But I'm no good . . ." I

stuttered. Milo du Peck had asked me to dance! I could feel my face getting hot.

"I'm sure if you dance anything like your grandad, you will be fabulous. Let your body feel the music," Milo said as he led me to the dance floor, where Wai Gong and Carmen were still wowing the crowd.

I closed my eyes for a second and imagined that YouTube Brian from New York was here with his big white toothy smile, telling me about the basic steps for the cha-cha. Forward, for-ward . . . back . . . back. It was all coming back to me now! Tyler was right—practice did make perfect. I did a chassé and moved my hips and worried I was horrible, but then I saw Wai Gong smiling, and I realized it didn't matter. Feeling self-conscious was holding me back.

"Brilliant!" Milo said.

Just then we were side by side with Wai Gong and Carmen.

"Swap?" asked Carmen, giving me a wink. "He wants to dance with you!" She twirled over to Milo, who spun me into Wai Gong's arms.

"KEEP DANCING!" they both shouted as they cha-cha'd away.

Wai Gong held me and grinned. "It's you and me now, Lizzie! Cha-cha-cha, tea-tea-tea!" He laughed. "Kam would be so proud to see you looking so lovely in your sparkly clothes. We're so proud of you, Lizzie!"

Dancing with Wai Gong felt easy. I'd known him all my

life and trusted him as he trusted me. We cha-cha'd around the floor. Instead of YouTube Brian being my dance coach, I had Wai Gong, who led like a professional. I imagined him and Grandma Kam in their youth, twirling around the floor. I knew she was here in spirit. I hadn't been able to feel her when we were out on the seafront, but now I knew she was with Wai Gong and me. Here we were, my grandad and me, two Chinese people on the floor of the Blackpool Tower Ballroom once again decades later.

I lost track of time for a while, and when the music stopped and I looked around, everyone was standing up and clapping. I thought they were clapping for Milo and Carmen. But they weren't on the dance floor anymore. It was only Wai Gong and me. They were clapping for us!

CHAPTER THIRTY-ONE

Blackpool Illuminations

When the evening was over, we went down to the street. This had been the best time ever. Wai Gong was elated. He looked up and down the road at all the Illuminations.

"I'm just going over there to see what those lights are," he said.

"Okay, but don't walk off," I told him. I followed him with my eyes just in case. I didn't want to have to save him from the sea or any trams that were going up and down the street.

"Was it all that you hoped for, Lizzie?" Chi asked. "You were amazing on that dance floor! Those YouTube classes really paid off."

"Yeah, it was magical."

"You were a star, Lizzie! And your grandad too!" said Tyler. "And you got to meet your *Strictly* idols. It's been such an incredible day. I'm so glad it was a success in the end."

"I'm just happy that we made it. It's been a long day for sure." I paused. "You know what though, I feel happy and a bit sad too."

"What do you mean?" Chi asked.

"The journey here made me realize a lot of things. Things are going to change a lot, and I'm not sure I'm ready," I said. I didn't know how to tell them exactly what I meant. I looked over to check on Wai Gong. He was staring up at a plastic pineapple light that was attached to the lamppost.

It was quite chilly now.

"What now?" I asked.

"I can call my parents to see where they are?" Chi said.

"Don't bother," Tyler replied. "They're already here."

A red-and-grey minivan pulled up beside us. The back door opened, and Minh hopped out.

"I think that's mine," he said, taking the camera off Tyler. "Sprout, you are in so much trouble. Be prepared to be grounded for a week."

Chi pouted.

"Chi Pham, how could you leave Minh?" Jane asked, getting out of the car. Tay got out too and joined us on the pavement. He gave Chi a big hug.

"We've been really worried about you, Chi," Jane said.

"Why are you dressed like the statue at my mum's house?" Tay added.

"Long story," Chi said. "Minh isn't an angel, Mum; this was all for a good cause. It was for Lizzie and her grandad."

Minh was looking at the footage while being annoyed with his kid sister. "You ditched me in the middle of nowhere. Even the biker ladies were in on it."

"I'm sorry, Minh. If you need to blame someone, blame me," I told him.

"Chi, we're here because you didn't tell us the truth about *you* bringing *Mr. Chu* here, not the other way around," said Jane. "We were disappointed to hear what you did. And we don't understand why you had to dress up. Minh mentioned something about Mr. Chu and a goddess?"

Chi took off the headdress and undid the hairpieces. "Tyler, can you pass me Lizzie's hoodie?" she asked. Tyler pulled it out of his backpack, and she put it on.

"Well, it's over now. I was only helping Lizzie for one day."

"I think Lizzie should tell you a bit more about why we came here," Tyler said.

I looked at Jane and Tay. "Well . . . Minh probably filled you in on some things. Chi was helping me out by dressing up as my grandad's favorite deity, Guan Yin. He thought Chi was the goddess, and he wouldn't come to Blackpool unless the goddess came." I took a deep breath. "I think he's got . . . dementia." I felt a crack in my throat as I tried to get the words out. "Whoa, it's hard to say these things out loud, isn't it?"

"Take your time to express what is in your heart," Tay said in his yoga voice.

"I didn't know what dementia was until one of the bikers mentioned her mum forgetting things," I said. "I thought Wai Gong was just grieving, you know, and that was the reason why he was acting all strange. But I think I knew deep down that something wasn't right. I just wasn't ready to admit it because then it might be real."

"Oh, Lizzie," said Jane. "I'm sorry to hear about your grandad."

"I thought we had been given a second chance when Grandma Kam left us the tickets for the Blackpool Tower Ballroom. I hoped he would go back to normal—and he did have a brilliant time—but it's obvious now that he needs more than a day trip. And I know I can't do this all by myself anymore."

"So you figured it out at the café when Dot started to talk about her mum forgetting things?" Minh asked.

I nodded. "I should have realized we were in trouble earlier."

A sadness poured over me. I choked back tears and wiped the corners of my eyes.

"Chi and I have been watching you struggle to fill your grandma's shoes these past six months," said Tyler. "We didn't know what we could do to help, but we're here for you."

"Yes, Lizzie," said Jane, giving me a hug. "You can count on all of us to be there for you. I know I'm tough on my own kids sometimes, as I want them to be independent. But I can see that you've had to grow up very early. Don't be afraid to ask for help. You can always turn to me."

Just then, Wai Gong came over to us. He was smiling. I wiped any sign of tears from my face.

"This is a very special place," he said.

"You're looking well, Mr. Chu," Tay said.

"Thanks . . . who are you?" Wai Gong asked. "You look familiar."

Jane and Tay looked at each other with concern. Wai Gong had known them for years.

"I'm Jane, and this is Tay."

"We've had such a good day, haven't we?" Wai Gong looked around at Chi, Tyler, and me. "Wait, where's Chi, your friend who used to eat roast dinners with us?"

"Roast dinners?" Jane asked, raising her eyebrows.

As if a lightbulb had gone on in his head, Wai Gong looked at me and blurted out, "Where's the goddess gone?"

I pointed at Chi, wondering if he would recognize her as my friend or the goddess.

"Mr. Chu, the goddess had to leave, unfortunately. She wanted you to know that you made lots of people very happy tonight when you dressed as Elvis," Chi said. She gave me a wink. I smiled. My friend seemed to have learned some compassion after all.

"Why are you all here?" asked Wai Gong, looking around at everyone. "Are we going home now?"

I took hold of Wai Gong's hand. "Yes, we can go home now," I said.

CHAPTER THIRTY-TWO

A Home Away from Home

The flat felt eerily quiet when we got back from Blackpool. Wai Gong and I were both exhausted. He went to bed, and I got ready for school the next day. I found the letter in the recycling that the school had sent when he hadn't shown up at parents' evening.

The next day, I told Mrs. Begum that I had been struggling with things at home and that's why I wasn't doing as well at school. She took me to meet with Mrs. Arnold, the head, who introduced me to Andrea Harris, the lady at school who helped kids with family things or personal matters. Jane came along too to be there with me.

Andrea was great and really kind. She said I could have asked for help earlier, that I didn't have to try to do everything myself. I told her that the trip to Blackpool had made me see that things weren't right with Wai Gong and that I couldn't control everything. I'd thought everything would suddenly get better, but I was wrong. What it had shown me was that I had brilliant friends who cared about me and that it was okay to ask for help. Instead of ignoring things, I had to face what life threw at me, just like the pilgrims in the story *The Journey to the West*.

"Lizzie, I know you didn't realize it, but you have been acting as a carer," said Andrea. "It's such a big thing you've been doing, you know—keeping the household running at such a young age, looking after your grandad, and going to school too. Do you know how brave you've been?"

"Me? Brave? No, I just did what I had to do. There was no one else to do all that stuff at home." If I hadn't done it, it wouldn't have gotten done. I thought again about how Chinese people often didn't ask for help. I was changing that now by talking about what had been going on. I felt relief that I finally had someone I could talk to about what I had been going through and that there were people here to help me.

Wai Gong had an assessment and some medical tests, and he ended up getting a social worker called Conrad, who was very friendly.

"Lizzie, your grandad isn't going to go back to how he once was, I'm afraid. The best thing for him now is to spend some weekends in a residential home so you and he can both get a rest," Conrad told me.

"A home? You mean a care home?" I asked.

"Yes, but we think we should start with just some week-ends, not full-time care. It's mainly to give you a break, some space and time of your own, so you can be a twelve-year-old and not have to worry about your grandad's care all the time. The Phams are happy to have you stay with them now that their son is moving out."

Minh didn't know how much he'd helped me on this journey. He'd driven us most of the way to Blackpool, and now he was going away to do his film course and was fine with me using his bedroom. I felt so grateful to him and the Phams.

Minh had made his documentary about our road trip to the Blackpool Tower Ballroom. He'd called it *Keep Dancing, Mr. Chu*. Tyler had filmed a lot of good stuff from the ball-room balcony, and Minh was especially happy with the shots we'd gotten on the beach. He'd gone back to Bamber Bridge to film the lady bikers some more, and he had interviewed Wai Gong and me in our flat. He made a mash-up of clips of when Wai Gong and I were dancing and gave me a copy on DVD for a keepsake.

"Here, Lizzie, have this as a memory of your journey to the west. Your grandad is really proud of you, even though some-times he doesn't know it."

Now that Minh didn't live at home, he and Chi got on well. I thought she missed him now. He took all his *Star Wars* things with him. And he got a new car—the Mini Orange had to be scrapped after our Blackpool trip. Obviously, we got the money from the backseat that Tyler had hidden before it was pulverized. Jane and Tay made sure we retrieved it the night we got back from Blackpool. I knew exactly what I wanted to use the money for. It was going to be for a gift for Wai Gong.

I enjoyed my weekends with the Phams. Chi was extremely happy, as the Pham weekly fare became more varied and included a little chicken and fish now, seeing as I wasn't a vegan. Chi said I should move in permanently now that Minh had moved out.

"That could actually happen, Lizzie," added Jane. "Only if you wanted it to though."

It was something to think about. I'd been going over to Chi's since I was little. I could imagine myself living there; Chi always had my back. Plus, Tyler and his dads said they would help out too and could take me to see Wai Gong whenever I wanted.

The weekends at the Phams' were fun, but I knew they wouldn't last forever. Something else would have to change soon. Things were getting harder at home. Wai Gong was forgetting more things; often he didn't even remember what foods he liked to eat, and he sometimes called me Kam. After I found him wandering the streets one day, confused, looking for Guan Yin, we knew the time had come to take him to a new permanent home.

It was the day of our first visit. The sign outside read CHERRY TREE CARE HOME.

The automatic doors startled Wai Gong. "There's nothing to worry about," said Adrian, one of the care home staff, patting him reassuringly on the arm. "Everyone will be happy to meet you, Jimmy."

I felt nervous for him, like he was starting at a new school or something. They wouldn't know how to make his tea or that he liked his toast nearly burnt or that he was the biggest *Strictly Come Dancing* fan in the whole of Glasgow. I'd packed the tartan shopping cart with some things for Wai Gong; I didn't care if Luke saw me using it. If he called me Old Lady Lizzie, I really didn't care anymore. I had even used the cart to move some of my stuff from the flat to the Phams' house. Shopping carts were given a bad reputation!

A tall man with bright red bushy hair came over to us. He was the care home manager, Thomas. "Hi there, welcome to Cherry Tree Care Home. We've heard a lot about you. We've made up your room, and Lizzie has brought some photos and comforts for you to make it feel like home."

Thomas told me Wai Gong wasn't allowed to burn his incense there, but he could offer oranges to his statues like he used to, so I'd gotten him a net bag of clementines. I'd also brought along a couple of other things that would make him feel better. I'd brought the dancing cat mug so he would know that being different was okay. And I had a surprise, which I had placed in a special box with polka dots on it.

Wai Gong's bedroom had peach wallpaper, and the sun would shine through the window in the mornings. It was bigger than the bedrooms we had at home. It had a small TV on a bracket on the wall and a velour armchair with high wings around the head so you could comfortably nod off to sleep. The floor was one of those easy-clean floors—no carpet—and the curtains were green with silver flowers on them. Outside was the communal garden. There were trees and birdbaths and some metal tables and chairs for residents. One lady was sitting out there in a wheelchair, a heavy blanket over her legs. She was wearing sunglasses even though there wasn't any sun.

Near the bed was a big orange button on a long wire. That was for calling the carers if Wai Gong needed help.

"Here are some of the activities we do," said Thomas. He handed me a leaflet. Tai chi and dancing would be good for Wai Gong. There were also arts and crafts, computer club, large textbooks, spa days, and outings to the local park.

"It looks great," I said. "Wai Gong, what do you think?"

"Oh, it's wonderful, isn't it, Lizzie? We'll be so happy here," Wai Gong said.

"No, Wai Gong. It's not for me. I'm not allowed to stay here with you," I said. I felt my chest get all tight. "I will come and visit you all the time. I'm not too far away. This will be your new home, remember how we talked about it with the goddess? She thinks it's the best place for you now." I wanted to cry, but I had to be strong for Wai Gong. This was the best place for him.

"I'm going to be here without you. But I don't want to be without my Lizzie," he said. "We're family, Lizzie. I don't want to be here alone."

"I love you, Wai Gong, and we are still family. Anytime you want to call me or have me come around, I will come. No worries. I will always be there for you."

Jane gave my arm a squeeze. "You're doing the right thing," she whispered. "He'll be fine, just give him some time."

I nodded.

"Mr. Chu, why don't I show you the garden?" said Thomas.

Wai Gong grinned; it was like he'd forgotten what we were just talking about. "Yes! The garden looked lovely. I never had a garden like this," he said.

Thomas led him out of the bedroom. I stood and watched them emerge outside. Wai Gong was animated as he looked around at the gnomes and the windmill water feature. Thomas was smiling and chatting with him, and Wai Gong seemed to be responding well.

"Are you all right, Lizzie?" asked Chi. "It's a big step for both of you, I know."

"I'm okay, I guess. Thanks for letting me stay with you," I said to Jane and Chi.

"You're part of the family now, Lizzie," Jane said. She handed me a set of keys. "These are for you."

I took out Wai Gong's set of keys with the Baby Yoda on them and transferred the little guy to the keys to my new home.

"Yes! Oh, I forgot about him," Chi said, linking arms with me. "We're gonna be sisters from another mother . . . or whatever that saying is."

"Lizzie!" Wai Gong called through the window. "Come here and sit with me on this bench."

I picked up the polka-dot box, went outside, and sat next to him. He took my hand and gently dropped the gold and jade necklace into my open palm.

"I got it back for you with the money from being that Elvis guy. He makes a lot of money!" Wai Gong laughed.

I gave him the biggest hug and put the necklace around my neck where it belonged. "Do you want me to tell you a story?" I asked him.

"I'd love it," he said. "It has to be a Guan Yin story though."

"Of course, how could it be a story about anyone else? Let's begin."

The Legend of Miao Shan

A long, long time ago, a king wanted to marry off his three daughters to suitors, but the youngest daughter—Miao Shan— wanted to be a nun instead. She wanted to spend her life helping people and knew that for her own good, she needed to be away from her father.

However, the king was stubborn and wanted things his way. He was angry, and he stopped speaking to her, which left the rest of his family broken and sad. After a while, he could no longer even look at her, so he banished her from his kingdom.

The king did not know that Miao Shan spent her time helping others.

Years later, the king became ill. Nothing and no one could help him recover. Yet one day, a monk arrived and told him that to get well, he must "take the potion from the person who sacrifices everything for love, someone who would give themself a thousand times over." The king did not know anyone so devoted to helping others. His older daughters had families of their own and were unwilling to help. The king was alone.

Miao Shan had devoted years and years to helping others and in doing so had transformed into a magical goddess upon Fragrant Mountain.

One day, the king had a visitor, a stranger who gave him a potion. Instantly, the king felt much better. The monk told him it was a potion made with love. The strange visitor had traveled thousands of miles to bring it. It was none other than his daughter, Miao Shan.

The king realized that his youngest daughter had chosen the path of compassion and kindness. He wept and asked for her forgiveness.

In a flash, Miao Shan was transformed into the goddess of one thousand arms and one thousand eyes, Guan Yin. Many arms for healing the world, and many eyes for seeing the suffering of the world.

I opened the polka-dot box and gave Wai Gong a new Guan Yin statue, one that was not broken in the middle. I'd used the money from the car wash to get it for him. It was bigger than the old one.

"I'm just a phone call away, Wai Gong, if you ever need me. I'll come see you just like Miao Shan."

"I love her so much, and I love you, Lizzie," Wai Gong said. "She hasn't come to see me in a while." He picked up the new Guan Yin statue and smiled. "I know just where to put this. Come on, Goddess, let's put you in my room by the window."

I touched the jade on the chain around my neck. I knew everything was going to be all right.

CHAPTER THIRTY-THREE

Keep Dancing, Lizzie Chu

"Get ready, it's starting!" said Wai Gong as he settled into the burgundy velour armchair. Chi's parents grabbed seats while Chi and I sat on the arms of Wai Gong's winged chair. He looked like a Chinese god himself, wrapped in a long navy dressing gown, flanked by two not-quite-immortal goddesses— Chi and me. Tyler was chatting with one of the old ladies, who was dressed in a frilly pink ball gown. Apparently, she wore it every Saturday night.

The familiar music began and the disco ball whirled on the screen. Everyone in the Cherry Tree common room was transfixed, except for a couple of residents who were already sleeping in their chairs. One had a crocheted blanket over her lap. Another cuddled a plastic doll dressed in a sleep suit.

I took out my phone and asked one of the care workers if she could take a photo of us all, because who knew when this would all change? Life had a habit of changing in the blink of an eye.

Even though we didn't live in the same house anymore, I felt like we were in a better place. It was like our family had expanded. Wai Gong could get the help he needed now, and I didn't always have to be the one looking out for him. I was so glad not to have to go to the market and drag food home or scour the aisles for yellow labels. I had my own social worker now called Layla, who was nice. She was young and didn't speak to me like I was a child. She had grown up in foster care, she said.

Tyler had taught Chi and me to sew squares, and we made blankets for the care home residents. I made a special one with sequins for Wai Gong. Chi was surprisingly good at it, as she had nimble fingers. I got people at school involved too, and we had a sewing circle every Friday afternoon for those who wanted to take part.

The presenters' dazzling teeth shone white on the screen.

"They look magical, don't they?" Wai Gong said. Chi and I grinned at each other. We'd had enough of fake goddesses and just wanted to spend some time in a grounded universe for a while. Being yourself was hard enough, and trying to be a totally new character was exhausting, as Chi had found out!

Wai Gong's memory was deteriorating, but one thing he could always remember how to do was dance! Luckily, at Cherry Tree, he had loads of people to dance with. They even had a tea dance every Thursday. He wouldn't be alone anymore. Neither would I.

Strictly Come Dancing was starting. We were all rooting for the children's TV presenter, who was eager to learn and seemed like a nice girl.

The first group dance began. Wai Gong stood and started clapping his hands.

One of the other residents, who looked youngish, came over and held out her hand. Wai Gong smiled. "Cha-cha?" She nodded.

"That's it, Jackie!" shouted someone sitting in the corner who I'd thought was asleep. Wai Gong and this Jackie lady began dancing.

"Everyone up! It's time to dance!" he declared.

Some of the residents began tapping their feet, and others sat clapping their hands. The staff smiled and joined in as the residents of Cherry Tree Care Home jived to Wai Gong's beat. Jackie went off to freestyle in front of the male carer who had just come into the room.

Then Wai Gong came over to me, patted my shoulder, and said, "Keep dancing, Lizzie!" He held out a hand to me, and I channeled my inner dancer and stood up. The cha-cha basics had cemented themselves in my memory. And we danced until it was time for me to go to my new home.

AUTHOR'S NOTE

I often get asked if my books are based on my life. I often say no—they are occasionally inspired by real people or events, but my main characters are not me. My books aren't exactly autobiographical. However, I have probably experienced the same emotions as my characters, as emotions are universal, and occasionally I might have been in similar situations.

I was a young adult carer in my early twenties. My mum, Jean, was a large woman, and she had her hips replaced. Unfortunately, both hip operations made her mobility worse, and often she couldn't walk without extreme pain. She could no longer work, go to the shops, or do the things many of us take for granted. I often took her out in a wheelchair.

When you are a child, you don't expect to have to look after your parents. I had to go to the post office and make sure the bills were paid. I had to bathe my mum and help her get dressed. I learned to cook all the foods my mum cooked for us and dealt with the GP and the hospital. At the same time, my dad, Ron, had clinical depression, which meant his mental health was very poor. He wouldn't get out of bed for weeks at a time.

Later, when my mum passed away, I was the main person responsible for my dad's care. I would visit him in the psychiatric hospital and take him food every day because he didn't like the food they had there. He later developed bipolar disorder, Parkinson's disease, and dementia. He thought some of his carers were a figure he called "Angel," and sometimes he would see this "Angel" when nobody was there. That is why I thought Wai Gong might see Guan Yin or talk to a goddess, as my dad used to do that, and he would wander off and make us all worried. I had to deal with social workers, carers, and medical staff, as he was in hospital every year. Many young carers have to deal with these things.

However, I didn't want this book to be about the struggles of being a young carer. I wanted it to be an uplifting story about love between family members, about asking for help. It's really about a granddaughter called Lizzie who has one amazing day with her grandfather (and her friends) before everything changes.

Occasionally, I felt resentful that I was a young adult carer and that having a regular life was difficult; sometimes I felt very sad. I was a young woman, and I wanted to have a fun life like my friends. At other times though, I felt very humbled by the experience, and it brought me closer to my dad. He always wanted to go to Australia, but I couldn't afford to take him, so instead I arranged a day out in Dublin, where they have the factory for his favorite drink, Guinness. We flew there, and he had such a brilliant day because he had never been on a plane before. I wanted to re-create that feeling of doing something nice for someone you love, and that is what happens in *Keep Dancing, Lizzie Chu*.

Keep dancing through life the best way you can, because sometimes life is hard!

ACKNOWLEDGMENTS

Well, what can I say! Writing this book during the pandemic was not easy. Nothing has been easy though, has it? We've all been through so much and continue to struggle. To the young people reading this, you've done so well. You've had to face a huge challenge, I'm so proud of you all.

I want to thank medical staff, teachers, and key workers of all kinds. Thanks to the TV and film crews who quarantined in bubbles to make entertainment for us when we were stuck at home. My lockdowns were made much brighter because of light entertainment like *Strictly Come Dancing*, hence this book!

Big thanks to my agent, Chloe Seager, and the team at the Madeleine Milburn Literary, TV, and Film Agency.

Without my publishers, there would be no book, so thanks to my editor, Erica Finkel, at Amulet Books and the Abrams Kids team—THANK YOU! Thanks also to Marie Oishi, Maggie Moore, Chelsea Hunter, Micah Fleming, Emily Daluga, Maggie Lehrman, and Andrew Smith.

Also, thank you to the cover artist: Natelle Quek, it's been so great working with you again! The cover shows Lizzie's journey so well.

I've had the most brilliant debut year and have a lot of people to thank:

The Goodshippers debut author group on Twitter! (You know who you are!) You've been fantastic! May your success continue. We survived our debut year in a pandemic!

To my DV Debut mentors, Kat Cho, Clairbel A. Ortega, plus Beth Phelan and the Diverse Voices Team—you've been great!

Early draft readers Joanne Lloyd, Ellen Boulton, Josh Simpson, Jasmine, and the always accommodating Lui Sit. Thanks to Lui's parents in Australia, who answered my questions about their love of ballroom dancing.

Thanks to those who answered questions for research:

David Sham and family for the Blackpool ballroom competition photos and information about ballroom and Latin dances.

Judith from Newham Chinese Community Centre, who talked about setting up the ballroom dancing club for fifty-through eighty-year-olds.

Gaynor Jones for sharing her photos, videos, and memories of Blackpool and the sound of the gulls!

Susan Brownrigg for brilliant Blackpool Tower information and general Blackpool knowledge and the full read.

To Chi Thai (Chi is named after you!), Ten The Gioi, Mai-anh Petersen, and Tuyen Nguyen for helping me with the British Vietnamese names and for answering my questions.

Mina Ali for information about social workers and looking after children.

Thanks to Waterstones Byres Road bookstore staff for not kicking me out when I was in there typing this story for hours at a time.

Thanks to Books of Wonder in New York and Blue Willow in Houston, who championed *Danny Chung Sums It Up* and let me be on awesome panels!

A big shout-out to the people of Glasgow. People really do make Glasgow. Thanks for being so welcoming!

Keep trying, keep laughing, keep dancing!

ABOUT THE AUTHOR

Maisie Chan is a British-born Chinese author. Her middle-grade debut, *Danny Chung Sums It Up*, won the Jhalak Prize and the Branford Boase Award, and it was on the Blue Peter Book Award shortlist. She also started the group Bubble Tea Writers to support and encourage new British East and Southeast Asian writers in the United Kingdom. When Maisie isn't writing, she enjoys yoga, dim sum, and singing really loudly. She has lived in the United Kingdom, the United States, and Taiwan. Originally from Birmingham, Maisie now lives with her family in Glasgow.